"The Judge looked over at a woman sitting at a table. He said, 'I sentence Miss Terri Geiger to one year at Hudsonville.'

"I gasped. Hudsonville. That's where they slashed the girls' throats. I couldn't take it.

"I screamed, 'Your honor, give me another chance.'

" ... He stared back ... 'I have no recourse but to send you away. It has to be that way.'"

Terri

John Benton

NEW HOPE
BOOKS

Fleming H. Revell Company
Old Tappan, New Jersey

ISBN:0-8007-8408-1
A New Hope Book
Copyright © 1981 by John Benton
All rights reserved
Printed in the United States of America
This is an original New Hope Book, published by
New Hope Books, a division of Fleming H. Revell
Company, Old Tappan, New Jersey.

TO Connie and Rick Adams,
our daughter and son-in-law, who
have answered God's call to become
vitally involved in helping our
needy girls

Terri

1

"Okay, Terri, this is what we'll have to do," Sylvia explained as she pointed. "We'll have to approach the house from the back—through those woods—because Mrs. Thompson left her front-porch light on. It's dark back there, and nobody'll see us or get suspicious."

My heart was thumping like crazy. I don't know why I'd ever let Sylvia talk me into something like breaking into a house. I'd never done anything this stupid in all my fifteen years. And as we stood in the shadows, looking at that spooky house, I knew one thing for sure. If I got out of this alive, I'd never do it again, ever!

As we picked our way through the underbrush, I whispered, "Sylvia, do you think we really ought to go through with this? I mean, the word around town is that Mrs. Thompson is crazy!"

"Of course she's crazy!" Sylvia responded. "That's why we're going to knock off her house. If she's in there, she probably doesn't have enough brains left to identify us. I tell you, this will be easier than I thought."

I wasn't thinking like that. "Listen," I protested, "if this woman is crazy, we'd better pick another house. I worry about crazy people; you never know what they'll do. In fact, my dad told me about one crazy woman. The authorities found out she'd murdered someone and cut that person's body up into small pieces and fed it to her cats!"

I shuddered at the utter horror of the idea.

"Oh, come on," Sylvia responded. "You don't believe those stories, do you? That's just a bunch of baloney parents make up to scare their kids."

"What do you mean, they make it up?" I answered, rising to my dad's defense. "I've read about those perverts in New York City, how they cut up the bodies of prostitutes."

Sylvia let out a low laugh. "For crying out loud, Terri, we're not prostitutes. We've got nothing to worry about."

Maybe she wasn't worried, but I sure was. And I was even getting sick from thinking about those cut-up bodies. What a horrible way to die!

Just ahead I could make out the outline of the three-story house. It was an old Victorian-style house, and it looked haunted. I knew that crazy woman had a bunch of cats and that we were going to end up as cat food!

I tried to keep Sylvia in sight as we moved through the woods. I was thinking that earlier that evening she had sounded so convincing when she had persuaded me to help her. She showed me some new clothes she had bought after her last burglary. When she told me how she did it, she seemed so excited. And it seemed so simple. But listening to someone tell about it and being involved were two entirely different things.

"Sylvia, you sure we're doing the right thing?"

She spun around and looked me straight in the eye. "What's the matter, Terri? You chicken?"

"Chicken? Never!"

"Then prove it. I don't want to hear one more question about whether or not this is the right thing to do. Trust me."

I never was one to back down from anything. But that didn't stop me from being scared. I had this feeling that something terrible was going to happen to me.

As we got to the edge of the woods, Sylvia stopped me and explained that we'd have to crawl on our stomachs up to the back door.

"Now, if for some reason we get caught," she said, "we're going to say we heard Mrs. Thompson has been starving her cats, and we just came to check it out. You understand?"

I wished she hadn't brought up cats—not while I was worrying about our becoming cat food!

"Suppose they don't believe us?"

"Terri, you are really stupid. You've got a lot to learn about knocking off houses. The first thing is always have an excuse. And it's best if that excuse has something to do with helping someone or a cat or a dog or something like that. People tend to believe your story if you have good intentions. But don't be stupid and tell them you were lost and trying to find your way home. That one's worn out!"

Sylvia was smarter than I thought. I knew her from school, but we had never been pals. Now we were getting acquainted better under these unusual circumstances. I couldn't help but wonder why she had offered to split fifty-fifty with me on this job. Why hadn't she picked out someone else?

Squirming back and forth on our stomachs, we inched toward that back door. It didn't look that far when we stood at the edge of the woods, but every foot we moved seemed as though it took an eternity.

When we got about halfway across the open space, a bloodcurdling scream pierced the air. I stiffened; my hair stood on end. Then I went straight up. I think my feet were already moving when I hit the ground, but before I could go anywhere, a hand grabbed my jeans and yanked me back down. I started to scream, but a hand clamped over my mouth. I fought determinedly, and then I discovered I was wrestling with Sylvia.

"Calm down," she whispered. "That's just Mrs. Thompson's way of trying to scare off prowlers."

"How do you know that?" I asked. "Maybe somebody is in there trying to kill her!"

"No, it's a decoy," Sylvia answered knowingly.

"Decoy? What are you talking about?"

"Okay, Terri, I haven't told you much about this caper, so I'll level with you. I have thoroughly checked this out. Not only is this woman crazy, but she's filthy rich."

I stared ahead at the house. Shutters hung at crazy angles all the way up to the third floor. Spooky shadows played across it. If she were rich, why did she live in a dump like this?

"You know Mr. Walden, the postman?" Sylvia went on.

"Yeah, but what's he got to do with all this?"

"Well, one day I was talking to him about that new movie, *Terror Strikes at Midnight.*"

I sure knew about that one. All the kids at school had been to see it. They said it was the scariest movie that had ever been made. I knew I wasn't going to see it. I couldn't stand horror movies; I couldn't sleep for weeks after watching one.

"Well, I told Mr. Walden about the movie one day," Sylvia continued. "Then get this, Terri. He leaned close and whispered that he knew of a house in town that is just like the spook houses in the movies. You know, ghosts, goblins, and everything like that. Can you imagine?"

I pointed toward Mrs. Thompson's house. "Are you trying to tell me this is a haunted house?"

Sylvia nodded. My heart slammed to my throat. It was bad enough robbing, but robbing a haunted house! No way was I going to do that!

I started to push up when Sylvia jerked me down

closer to her. "Wait, Terri; you haven't heard the whole story. I want you to hear something else Mr. Walden told me."

"That she cuts up people and feeds them to her cats?"

"No, stupid. Get off that cat trick."

"Well, what did Mr. Walden tell you?"

"He told me Mrs. Thompson is filthy rich. She is loaded with money and jewels and everything like that."

"How does he know?"

"He made me promise I'd never tell," Sylvia said, "but I think I can trust you. Promise not to tell?"

I promised, but I really didn't mean it. Mostly I was dying of curiosity.

"Well, she's on his route, too. He says he knows all about everybody on his route by the mail they receive. The dirty old men get *Playboy,* and the dirty old women get *Playgirl.*"

I giggled.

"And that's not all. Mrs. Thompson gets fat envelopes from banks and from people who deal in bonds and securities. Mr. Walden says that this old girl has money, and I do mean m-o-n-e-y!"

What I still couldn't figure out was if she had all that money, why did she live in a dilapidated house in this neighborhood?

"That's not all," Sylvia went on. "He also delivers lots of boxes from famous jewelry stores. He thinks she keeps all the jewelry stashed somewhere in the house."

"You're kidding! Mr. Walden wouldn't lie to you, would he?"

"Come on, Terri. You know him. He's a nice man. Why would he lie about something like that?"

"Well, just because he's a postman doesn't mean he always tells the truth, Sylvia. I'll bet the whole thing is a big lie."

I didn't know if it were or not. But I wasn't at all excited about getting involved in this caper now, so I was ready to try to convince Sylvia we ought to call it off.

"Come on, Terri. What's wrong with you? I give you an opportunity to help me get into one of the biggest heists anybody has ever pulled off. I mean, you and I are going to have money, baby. We're going to be rich!"

Money was something I could understand. We never had enough of it at home—especially with my dad's drinking all the time.

Just then another bloodcurdling scream from the house split the night air. Instinctively I bolted for the woods, and I heard Sylvia right behind me this time. Just as I was about to reach the safety of the woods, I felt something hit my legs, and I fell in a heap. Then I realized Sylvia had tackled me.

"I can't go through with this," I protested. "That woman is in there screaming. I'll bet she saw us. I'll bet she's waiting with a knife in her hand. As soon as we go through that door, she's going to stab us. She may even start cutting us to pieces before we're dead!"

"For crying out loud, Terri, your imagination sure works overtime," Sylvia said in disgust. "I told you that's nothing but a decoy. And let me tell you something else about rich people. Some rich people like to give others the idea they're crazy. Now take a look at that house." She pointed.

"Suppose you were Mrs. Thompson," she went on. "Suppose you were filthy rich. Wouldn't you be just like her? You wouldn't fix up your house because you would want everyone to think you were poor. Then they wouldn't try to rob you."

Sylvia had a point.

"You'd also want people to think you were a little off your rocker, too. Maybe you'd yell like that every once in a while. But that Mrs. Thompson's not fooling me."

Sylvia was making a lot of sense. I guess if I were rich and didn't want anyone to know it, maybe I'd live in a broken-down house, too. Maybe I'd scream to scare people off. Yes, Sylvia was smart. I'd better listen to what she told me.

"Let's go get all those millions of dollars and glittering diamonds," Sylvia said, rubbing her hands together in anticipation.

We got back down on our stomachs and started slithering toward our objective—the back door. But even thinking of all that money and jewelry didn't stop that gnawing fear inside. I still felt that something terrible was about to happen. Maybe there really were ghosts protecting this house!

As we got close to the house, I realized that the lawn was quite wet. "Sylvia," I whispered, "I'm getting all wet from this grass. Can we stand up and walk?"

"Keep down, stupid!" she sputtered. "You stand up, and you'll be easy prey for a shotgun blast."

That made me try to melt into the ground. Wet grass was a lot better than hot lead! Maybe this was what I was fearing. Maybe that old lady was standing behind that darkened window aiming her gun at us right now!

"I guess the only thing then is to get wet and muddy," I said, trying to take this development in stride.

Sylvia didn't answer. She just started wiggling forward again. I followed, but the grass seemed wetter than ever. That was strange because it had been several days since it rained.

I grabbed Sylvia's foot and whispered, "Something's wrong here. This looks like a setup! When they catch us, all they have to do is point to our wet clothes and to this wet grass. They'll know immediately we were crawling along here to knock off this house. I say it's a trap, Sylvia; it's a trap!"

She stared over at me looking a little startled. "You

may be right, Terri," she said thoughtfully. "It could be a setup."

We both looked toward the house. I thought I saw a figure walk by the window.

"Let's get out of here!" I whispered.

"No, hold it!" She started looking around.

"What are you looking for? You think she dropped some diamonds out here, Sylvia?"

"No, I was just thinking this grass may be mined."

"Mined?" I was on my knees now, and my teeth chattered wildly—partly from the chill of being wet and partly from sheer terror at the idea of sitting right in the middle of a minefield! "You mean she could set off a mine? A big blast? Like something that could blow us both to smithereens?"

Sylvia nodded, not appearing too concerned over the situation. Then she grabbed me and pointed toward the house. "Look over there."

I peered through the darkness but couldn't see anything where she was pointing.

"Look closely under that window, the other side of that bush. Look closely. Listen."

So help me, I couldn't see or hear anything out of the ordinary.

"See the water coming out the end of the hose?" Sylvia said. "It's streaming this way. Someone forgot to shut off the water. That's all it is."

I raised up ever so slightly and squinted. Sure enough, water was draining out of the hose and collecting in a low place where we now were.

Sylvia and I both heaved sighs of relief. "It's not a setup," she announced.

"But what about the mines?" I asked.

She laughed under her breath. "Just trying to scare you. I like to do things to help people remember their first burglary."

Oh, how I wanted to smack her in the mouth! This was no joking matter. I still felt imminent danger. And I was sure I had seen someone at that window.

Sylvia surveyed the ground and announced, "It's drier over to the right. Let's move that way."

As we got to the back door, Sylvia reached for the crowbar she carried in her jeans. But I noticed that the door was slightly ajar. When I pointed that out to her, she said, "That looks suspicious."

"What do you mean?" I asked as once again my heart jumped into my throat.

"Well, I'm not trying to scare you now; it's just something you need to know. Sometimes people will leave the door slightly open as a trap. When you push it open, it triggers either an alarm or a bomb. I read about it in a detective magazine."

I shuddered at the idea of being blown to bits by a booby trap. But then I remembered the cats. "Hey," I said, "I got it. Maybe she left the door open so her cats can come and go. That way she doesn't have to get up and let them out during the night."

"You must be crazy, Terri. No woman who is filthy rich and lives alone is going to leave her door open like that. If she's got money and jewelry in there, she'll keep her doors locked. This doesn't make sense."

"What are we going to do?" I wailed.

"Let me think."

She kept staring at the door, then finally started crawling to the right. When I started after her, she said, "No, you stay here. I'll be right back."

Where in the world was she going? Here I was at the bottom of the stairs all by myself. I was trembling from head to toe. Oh, how I wanted to jump up and tear out of there. But I didn't want to risk getting shot in the back. I'd better wait.

A few minutes later Sylvia came crawling back. "Find anything?" I asked.

"No, not a thing," she responded. "I wonder if it's for the cats like you said or if it's a trap. We've got to find out."

"But how?"

"Terri, you crawl up the stairs and push the door ever so gently. That's all."

I looked over at her wide-eyed. "Sylvia, you must think I'm nuttier than Mrs. Thompson! All you want is for me to go up and test the door. If it's a booby trap, I know who's going to be blasted to smithereens! I may be dumb, but I'm not stupid!"

Sylvia didn't respond. Was she just testing me to see how far along I'd go? Had she brought me along to get me killed? Suppose we got in there and got millions of dollars in cash and diamonds. Would she try to kill me so she could have it all? I had heard somewhere that there's no honor among thieves. And I was finding it out firsthand!

"You're right, that was a stupid idea I had," she finally said. "But I've got another one—if I can find what I need. You stay here."

Once again she crawled away around the corner of the house. Maybe I really should take off. Maybe she was planning to make me the patsy for this whole crime. But visions of all that money kept me in position. It was so tempting. . . .

In a couple of minutes she came crawling back, carrying a long stick.

"What in the world is that for?" I asked.

"You're still a dummy, Terri," she responded. "Watch."

She proceeded to take the stick, shove it toward the door until it was touching it, and then push gently. The door's hinges squeaked, just like in the movies. Sylvia pushed a little harder.

She pushed and pushed until finally the door was wide open. I stared into the darkness. I could see nothing behind that door—no cats, no Mrs. Thompson. But I still had that uneasy feeling. Why should we be so lucky as to find the door unlocked? It was almost as though someone were inviting us in.

Sylvia must have felt the same way, for instead of starting up the steps, she whispered, "Something's terribly wrong here. It's too easy."

Just then a cat scrambled out the door and tore on by us. Startled, we both jumped. Then I realized that cat was jet black. Maybe this place really was haunted!

Sylvia grabbed me and commanded, "Follow me," as she started up the steps.

"You must be the crazy one!" I protested. "That open door is an invitation to something terrible."

Sylvia began to meow softly like a cat. Then she whispered to me, "Make a noise like a cat. We're Mrs. Thompson's cats coming back home."

So with both of us meowing like crazy, we crawled inside. When I looked around, I realized we must be in the kitchen. I couldn't see much, but I could feel the newspapers all over the floor. I figured she must have put those down for the cats, and I made a mental note that I'd better be careful where I crawled!

From the looks of that kitchen, I guess it was appropriate for Sylvia to say that Mrs. Thompson was filthy rich. I still wasn't sure about the rich part though.

Just then that bloodcurdling scream pierced the air again. It sounded even worse inside and seemed to be coming from the living room. I had started out the back door when Sylvia grabbed my foot. "Stay here," she said, "and I'll check it out."

I was trembling and couldn't move even if I wanted to.

I watched Sylvia disappear into the living room. Nervously, I waited. What if whatever was in there got her and then came looking for me? What would I do if she didn't return? Would I dare go looking for her? The more those possibilities crossed my mind, the faster my heart beat.

Then I spotted Sylvia in the doorway motioning for me to come. "You've got to see this," she said. "You won't believe me."

I followed her to a corner of the living room. The porch light reflected off the walls and enabled us to see a little. This room was filthy, too—more papers all over. And it smelled horrible. This must have been the main bathroom for the cats.

Sylvia pointed toward a small table in the corner and motioned for me to stand up, too. There on the table was a small cassette recorder with a tape running through it. Just then there was another bloodcurdling scream. I jumped, and Sylvia laughed. That scream came from the recorder! Mrs. Thompson was using modern technology in her attempts to frighten away intruders!

"Can you imagine that?" Sylvia said, almost in awe. "I'll bet the old bat is gone for the night, so she left this recording on as a decoy. People hear the screams and think she's at home. But it's just a recording."

I nodded.

"Let's get started looking," Sylvia said. "She's nowhere around tonight. How could we ever be so lucky?"

She moved across the living room and opened a door which led into a bedroom. She went in and started rummaging around.

I decided I'd better keep close to her. I had never robbed a house before and hadn't the foggiest notion of where to look for valuables. My folks never had anything worth hiding!

Sylvia had me help her pull the mattress off onto the floor. "Usually they hide money underneath the mattress," she said. But we didn't find anything.

She grabbed a drawer from a dresser, turned it upside down onto the floor, and started rummaging through the contents. "That old lady must have it hidden well," she complained. "There's nothing here."

She dumped out the other drawers and then headed for the closet. I followed, and she told me to check the pockets—especially coat pockets. Once again, nothing.

"Check the shoes," she said.

I ran my fingers up into the toes of those shoes. It felt so creepy. Suppose I ran into a spider. Spiders went with an old house like this. Or maybe she had mousetraps in the closet. I slowed my search—just in case.

Sylvia wasn't letting anything slow her down. But when our search ended up a total zero, she started to cuss. "Where does that old lady keep all her money?"

Just then I heard a car in her driveway. Was she coming home? Would she catch us red-handed in her house? I ran to the bedroom window and peered out. But I saw more than just a car in the driveway! I saw red lights on top of the car!

"It's the cops!" I whispered in total terror.

2

I bolted for the living room. I was getting out of this trap!

But just as I turned the corner into the kitchen, a light flipped on. There stood an old woman with a shotgun leveled at me.

"Stop, or I'll blow your brains out!" she shouted.

I threw my hands up in the air. "I've got nothing on me!" I screamed. "Have mercy!"

Taking a step forward she demanded, "Where's your friend?"

Sylvia! Where was she? I thought she'd be right behind me. Hadn't she heard what I said when I saw those cops? Maybe she was hiding. I'd better play it cool for her sake.

"What friend?" I responded. "Who says I have a friend?"

"Listen, you little twerp," the old woman snarled, "I ought to kill you!"

I noticed her finger as she pulled the hammer back to cock the shotgun. She meant business!

"My friend jumped out the window and took off through the woods," I lied.

"Well, I'm going to tell you something, little girl. She probably got electrocuted. You're lucky I didn't electrocute you when you crawled across that wet spot on the lawn."

I looked down at my jeans and blouse. They were still pretty wet.

"You see, little girl," the old woman went on, "I have electrical wires hidden all through my property. When I saw you and your friend coming up, I pulled the switch and waited. You took so long getting in that I had plenty of time to call the police. I knew you two were coming to rob me, you dirty little thieves. Well, you're lucky to be alive still. If I had left that switch on, there'd be nothing left of you but a little pile of ashes. Nobody would ever know what became of you. You'd be just another missing-person statistic." She cackled like a witch.

Once again I was shaking from head to foot. I wondered about Sylvia. I didn't think she had taken off. But where was she? How could I warn her not to run across that yard?

Just then a cop came bursting in through the back door at about the same time another came in through the front door. Then I realized why the doors were unlocked. She had unlocked them so the cops could get in.

When that cop spotted me with my hands still raised to the ceiling, he said, "Oh, you already got one, Mrs. Thompson? Good work. I'll take over from here. You can put the gun down."

The cop grabbed my arm, spun me around, and demanded, "What's your name?"

I had had no experience in dealing with cops. Should I give him a false name? Would he beat a confession out of me?

"I'm Sylvia Geiger," I said, so scared that I didn't realize I had used Sylvia's first name and my own last name.

"Sylvia Geiger? You're not Harold Geiger's kid, are you?"

I nodded but couldn't help but wonder how this cop

knew my dad. Dad hated cops.

"I caught your dad drunk a couple of weeks ago," he went on. "He's a friendly enough guy when he's drunk, so I didn't arrest him. I just took him home and warned him that the next time I'd have to take him in and book him."

So that was the car that pulled up in front of our house a couple of weeks ago. When Dad staggered in, he said his friend had brought him home. But it was this cop!

Just then the other cop came in from the living room, marching Sylvia in front of him. "I found this one hiding in the closet," he announced.

The cop holding me asked Sylvia her name. She tightened her lips. Then it hit me what I had done. I had used her first name. I should have said my name was *Terri Geiger,* not *Sylvia Geiger.* Now I'd probably fouled things up for both of us.

When Sylvia wouldn't answer, the cop said, "Okay, have it your way. Let me read you your rights." He said we could make one phone call. That would be stupid. The only person I knew to call would be my parents, and they would be furious with me.

Sylvia already was handcuffed. Now they handcuffed me. Those things hurt, and they felt horrible. This was my first time—and I hoped it would be my last. If I got out of this mess. . . .

As the cops started us out toward the patrol car, Mrs. Thompson kept watching us closely. And she kept the gun ready to aim at us if we tried anything. The cops just seemed to ignore her.

As the cop pushed me into the car, I whispered, "Don't you know that Mrs. Thompson is a nut?"

He laughed. "Of course I know it. That's why we hurried over here. She keeps threatening to kill people who come to rob her. Seems like a lot of people think she's wealthy. If they only knew. She's on welfare."

I looked at Sylvia, and she looked at the cop. Had we been fooled?

"Hey, Terri, should I tell this joker who this Mrs. Thompson really is?" Sylvia asked.

When Sylvia mentioned my real name, I stiffened. Would the cop catch the slip?

He caught it. "I thought your name was *Sylvia Geiger,*" he said. "How come your partner called you *Terri?* Did you give me a false name?"

Sylvia just stood there. Why didn't she cover for me?

Finally I said, "I'm sorry, officer. My name is really *Terri Geiger,* not *Sylvia.* I guess I just got nervous and used Sylvia's name."

Sylvia glared at me. Oh, no! Now I had given away her first name! Dumb me!

"Well, we're finally getting the story straight," the cop said. "You're Terri Geiger, and the other girl is Sylvia. But what's Sylvia's last name?"

"Okay, okay, you'll probably find out anyway," Sylvia said. "I'm Sylvia Bolden."

"It doesn't make any difference really," the cop responded. "We're going to take you both down and book you for burglary."

"Hey, it's not what it looks like, officer," Sylvia said. "Terri and I heard that Mrs. Thompson has been starving her cats to death. All we did was come to check out the story. We were going to report her to the Humane Society."

The cop slapped his thigh and heehawed. "I suppose you were checking all those drawers for cats, hey? Did you find any cats hidden under that mattress you pulled onto the floor?"

I knew they had us, so I kept my mouth shut. Probably Sylvia would have been better off if she hadn't tried that stupid excuse.

The officer started to push Sylvia in beside me when Mrs. Thompson appeared with her shotgun leveled right at all of us. I held my breath. Was that crazy lady going to kill us right here before the police?

"Stop! Stop!" she called. "You, officers, stop!"

"What's the matter, Mrs. Thompson?" one of the officers asked kindly.

"I've changed my mind! I've changed my mind. I've decided to let these two little girls go free. I'm not going to press charges against them."

"Now, Mrs. Thompson," one of the officers soothed. "It's nice of you to be so generous. But we caught these young ladies red-handed. We really ought to take them down and book them. All you'll have to do is appear at their trial to testify against them. Maybe if these two do a little time for this burglary, it will deter them from a life of crime."

"Hey, cop, can't you understand plain English?" Sylvia said sarcastically. "The lady said to let us go!"

He turned toward Sylvia and shouted, "You shut up before I shut you up."

He turned back toward Mrs. Thompson and pleaded, "Please do what I say. It's for the best."

The old lady pointed the gun straight at the cop and yelled, "I said, 'Let those two little girls go.' As far as I'm concerned, they were just walking down the street. Now unlock those handcuffs! I'm not going to press charges!"

The cop looked at his partner, shrugged, and said, "What can I do, Benny? Let them loose."

He yanked me out of the car, and Benny undid our handcuffs. His partner was telling Mrs. Thompson, "So help me, the next time you call us, we're going to come like snails. This is ridiculous!"

"I know what I'm doing," Mrs. Thompson snarled. "Now get out of here before I call the mayor!"

The cops jammed the handcuffs into their belts,

jumped into their car, and backed out far too fast. I could tell they were furious at Mrs. Thompson.

Right now the thrill of being free was tempered with a new worry. Now that the officers were gone, would she kill us? She still had her gun aimed at us.

"I'm terribly sorry for what happened," Sylvia started in. "And I promise you it'll never happen again."

Mrs. Thompson didn't answer. She simply pointed the gun up into the air and pulled the trigger. At that deafening noise I bolted for the woods. I didn't worry about Sylvia pulling me down this time; she was ahead of me! I was hoping we'd get to the safety of the woods before I felt a shot in the back!

We both hit the woods going at top speed. The branches slapped my face and stung, but I still plunged ahead. Other than the noise we were making, crashing through the woods, the night was silent. We heard nothing further from Mrs. Thompson.

We ran until we were both completely out of breath. "I can't go on!" I gasped, collapsing to the ground.

"I can't, either!" Sylvia responded, falling to her knees beside me.

I looked back in the direction we had come. I really didn't expect that old lady to be chasing us through the woods, but you never know. But I saw nothing and heard only our labored breathing.

"Whew, that was close!" Sylvia finally said between gasps. "I just can't believe we got away! I must be dreaming!"

"It's no dream," I answered, rubbing my cheeks where the branches had slapped my face.

"I guess robbing a crazy woman has its advantages," Sylvia went on. "But was I ever scared that she was going to blast us to smithereens—and those cops along with us. Wasn't that a sight?"

"Sylvia, why did she let us go?"

She laughed and told me, "You have to understand, Terri. That woman is nuts. I mean, real nuts. I'll bet she thought if she let us off, we'd come back again. So she's playing a cat-and-mouse game with us. Being a nut, she probably enjoys all the drama of the cops, the guns, and all the rest."

"Well, let me tell you something about her place," I said. "She told me the whole place is wired. She said she turned the electricity off when we crawled across that wet spot on the lawn. If that electricity had been on, we would have been electrocuted and reduced to a pile of ashes. And nobody would ever know what happened to us!"

"She told you that?" Sylvia asked.

"She sure did. When she caught me in the kitchen."

Sylvia laughed. "You don't believe that big story, do you? Why, that's illegal. People can't use electrical charges like that. She'd be arrested!"

"You think she was lying?" I asked. "I'll bet she wasn't. Since she's crazy, she might think she could get by with something like that."

"Well, maybe you're right," Sylvia said. "I was just thinking about that fake scream, the shotgun, and her letting us go. It would be a perfect setup for someone to get electrocuted. But if somebody got hurt by a shock on that wet grass, it sure would go hard for Mrs. Thompson. The law wouldn't stand for that."

Bad for Mrs. Thompson? What about whoever got electrocuted? I knew I'd never try crawling across her lawn again. There was too much risk trying to rob a crazy person. Sylvia and I were lucky to be alive.

After a few minutes' rest we got up and made our way back to the main road. I had had enough for one night. Or so I thought.

I told Sylvia good-bye and walked the mile to our house. It wasn't very late yet. I guessed my folks would be surprised I had gotten in so early.

But when I walked up the steps to our front door, I heard loud arguing inside. Mom and Dad were at it again.

I threw open the door, and there was Dad on the floor with Mom on top of him, slapping him around. Mom was a big, fat slob, and Dad was small for a man. I guessed Dad was drunk again. They always got into a fight when he came home drunk, and Dad always lost.

"Mom, for crying out loud, don't hurt him!" I yelled.

She looked up but didn't get up. "I told him the next time he came home drunk, that would be it!" she yelled back. "I'm going to beat him so bad he'll never do this again!"

She doubled her fist and smacked him, *pow,* right in the eye! "He'll have a nice black eye to remind him of this close encounter!" she yelled, laughing derisively. "Now maybe he'll never drink again."

I didn't know whether to laugh or cry. The whole scene was totally ludicrous. Mom weighed at least 250 pounds—at least that's what she weighed when she went off her last diet about six months ago. Dad weighed about 135 and stood about five-feet-seven-inches tall in shoes. I never could understand what the two of them ever saw in each other in the first place.

While Mom's attention was diverted, Dad tried to take a swing at her. But he was too drunk to aim straight, and he was too small to hurt her even if he did aim straight. All he did was succeed in making her angrier.

She came down hard on his face again with her fist. She didn't miss, and Dad screamed in agony. She let him have another one right on the jaw.

"Terri, get this two-ton monster off me!" Dad shouted. "She's about to kill me!"

I ran over, grabbed Mom by the shoulders, and pulled her off-balance. She tumbled off Dad and rolled across the floor, her blubber making squishy noises as she rolled.

"Terri, I should have let him have it a few more times!" she screamed at me. "That man's drinking is driving me crazy. And it's going to be driving you crazy, too, when you hear what he's done this time. He spent every penny of our grocery money for liquor!"

"Every penny?"

"Every last, lousy penny. Why I ought to. . . ."

She struggled to get up but had to roll over toward the sofa to get some leverage. By that time she had forgotten her threat. It just took too much energy for her to get back on her feet, so she plopped into a chair.

Poor Dad. He was still holding his face in agony. I'm sure he must have been in terrible pain as he thrashed back and forth on the floor.

"Mom, beating on Dad won't get rid of his alcoholism," I protested. "What—"

"Alcoholism, bunk!" she interrupted. "He's a plain, ordinary drunk. And I hate drunks!"

"Mom, what Dad needs is. . . ."

This time I couldn't finish the sentence because I really couldn't think what it was he needed. I wasn't old enough to have all the answers to alcoholism.

Mom didn't care what he needed. She pushed and pulled her way out of the chair and stumbled toward the kitchen, mumbling, "I'm hungry."

No wonder she was really enraged at Dad for spending the grocery money. Mom had to have food as much as Dad had to have booze. They were both addicts.

I walked over to Dad, knelt down, and massaged his arms a little. He took his hands away from his face. I could see that Mom had really hurt him. He looked like he'd been knocked out in a boxing ring.

"Terri, believe me, I didn't mean to spend our grocery

money," Dad started in. He was always so apologetic
about everything when he was drunk. At least he didn't
get violent the way some drunks do. If he did, Mom
would probably have killed him before now.

"I was just going to stop for one little beer on the way
home after I got my check cashed. Then I had two beers.
And then, well, before I knew it the bartender wouldn't
sell me anything else because I didn't have any more
money. I must have had a little too much, huh?"

A little smile played across his bruised face. He was
like a little boy who'd gotten caught with his hand in the
cookie jar.

"Dad, you know better than that," I said to him, like a
parent correcting a child. "Don't ever drink up our grocery money."

He sat up and looked at me. "I'll tell you what, Terri,"
he said, his speech slurred. "I promise I won't eat for
thirty days. That way we'll say that my drinking was instead of eating. Okay?" He giggled.

I went to the bathroom, soaked a washcloth in cold
water, came back, and laid it on Dad's face.

As I touched his eye with the cold cloth, he reacted.
"Ouch!" he yelled. "That really hurts!" And he lay back
down on the floor to hold the cloth in place.

He looked so pitiful lying there. If he didn't have this
problem with liquor, he'd probably be the best dad in
the whole world. I always did like him. And he liked
me—maybe because I was an only child. But I knew his
drinking was driving him to an early grave. He had already had his driver's license taken away by the courts
and had to ride the bus to work. That embarrassed him
greatly. I often wondered if maybe his size and Mom's
treatment of him weren't his biggest problems. He had
never learned to adjust to his limitations. Drink was his
escape from reality.

I couldn't keep track of the number of jobs he had

had and lost because of his alcoholism. He was a good mechanic—when he was sober. He had a job now at Lazaar's, but even there they had suspended him for a week for being drunk on the job. He stayed home and stayed drunk that whole week.

"Terri, do you know where we can get some money?" Dad asked.

Why had he asked that? Had that cop already been to our house and told him about my being involved in that attempted robbery? Did Dad suspect what I had been doing?

"Dad, I wouldn't know anywhere in the world to get money," I answered, trying to throw him off the track. "Except maybe at a bank. You want me to rob a bank?"

He giggled. Then his face got that serious look as he went on, "Terri, we've got to get some money. I don't have a penny to my name. I don't get paid again for another month. Mom says we're out of groceries. She was planning to go shopping when I brought my check home tonight." He took the cloth from his eye and looked straight at me. "Terri, if we don't get some money, we're going to starve!"

I stared at him. Did he really mean that? I didn't remember him ever saying anything like this before. And what he said all fit together. Mom and I had cleaned up all the leftovers for supper tonight before Dad came home. But I didn't know the cupboards were bare.

"Come on, Dad," I said, "you're being overly dramatic. We've got some things to eat around here. We'll make it until your next paycheck."

"No we won't, Terri. There's no money or food in this house." He looked at me with his most pitiful look and said, "Can we borrow what you've got saved in your piggy bank? I know you were saving up for a special dress for the prom, but I'll get paid before then and will pay you back so you can get your dress."

"Dad," I said in shock, "you're too late. I bought that dress the day before yesterday. And it took every penny I had saved. There's nothing in my bank!"

"What?" Mom yelled from the kitchen. "You don't have any money, either?"

I walked out to the kitchen where she was sitting at the table. "Look at this sandwich!" she told me. "All I've got for a sandwich is lettuce—no meat, no eggs, no nothing. Just lettuce and mayonnaise and two slices of bread. And this is it, Terri. There's nothing left in the fridge."

I jerked open the refrigerator door. She was absolutely right. The only thing in there was about an inch of mayonnaise in a jar. And I couldn't stand mayonnaise.

I had been figuring on a little snack before I went to bed. I wasn't all that hungry, but the prospect of not having food in the house for a month was beyond my imagination. I slammed the refrigerator door and stomped back to where Dad was still stretched out on the living-room floor. I stepped across him and headed outside. I knew one thing for sure: I wasn't about to starve! I'd get money by hook or by crook.

The only store open this time of night was an all-night grocery about a mile from where we lived.

Cars kept passing me as I walked along, and finally one stopped. It was a man—alone. Maybe he would try to rape me! I was scared, but I was also conniving. I figured maybe I could get him—steal his wallet or something. Then I'd take the money back home so we could have food.

He rolled down the window and called, "Terri, want a ride?"

How did he know my name? I ran up toward the car, and he called out, "It's me, Pastor Gossman, from the Community Church. Can I take you somewhere?"

No wonder I didn't recognize him. My dad said he

thought I should go to Sunday school and took me to the Community Church a couple of times years ago. But Dad didn't like the church, and we never went back. Pastor Gossman had visited us to try to get us to come back, but nothing he said had worked. I guess somehow he must have kept up with our family because he recognized me.

"Sorry, I didn't know who it was," I told him. "That's why I hesitated. But, yeah, I do need a ride to the late-night grocery store."

As we drove along, I wondered what I was going to tell him I was going after. I just couldn't bring myself to admit that our family needed money for food. One thing that infuriated Dad was for me to talk about our family's business outside our home. And yet, weren't preachers supposed to help the poor? I guess part of the problem was that I had too much pride to admit we were poor.

"What did you run out of that you had to be out this time of night?" Pastor Gossman asked.

"Oh, Dad has a splitting headache," I replied, realizing as I said it that it was indeed true. "We were out of aspirin, and I told him I'd go get some."

"That's thoughtful of you," the pastor said. "Is your dad still having a big battle with his drinking?"

Don't tell me everybody in town knew about Dad. That was one of the problems in living in a small town like Kent. Everybody knew everybody else's business. That was one of the things that made it rough on me at school.

But still Kent wasn't a dinky town. I guess the last census showed we had almost ten thousand people. Surely everybody didn't know.

"Oh, no, Dad kicked the drink habit," I lied. "But he told me tonight that his headache was so bad that if he didn't get some aspirin right away, he'd be forced to take

a drink. That's when I flew out of the house on this mission of mercy. I don't want anything to give him the excuse to start drinking again."

"Well, your dad's stopped drinking," the pastor said
in surprise. "I think that's great!"

As we pulled up into the parking lot of the grocery
store, Pastor Gossman said, "Terri, it's getting pretty
late. I hate for a young girl like you to be walking
around alone at night. Why don't you go get those aspirin. I'll wait for you and drive you home. Okay?"

This would never do. "Oh, that's so thoughtful of
you," I responded. "But I just went out for the track
team at school. I'm supposed to jog a couple of miles
every day, and I haven't jogged today. I was really planning on jogging home. I'll be okay. But thanks. That's
sure nice of you."

"See you at church!" the pastor called as I jumped out
of the car.

Me, at church? I thought. *No way!* I didn't need that
stuff. That was for people who couldn't handle their own
lives.

I headed inside the store even though I didn't have
enough money to buy even a book of matches. But I had
to be sure that Pastor Gossman was gone.

The clerk recognized me and nodded. Then I realized
I had blown it. How could I rob this place now? The
clerk would be able to identify me immediately. Somehow I had to get some money. But how?

Then a wild thought hit me. Maybe I could sell my
body, like prostitutes do. I'd read somewhere about how
much money prostitutes made. I didn't like the idea, but
I sure needed the money. But I had no idea of how to go
about being a prostitute. I mean, what do you say? What
do you do? I knew we had a red-light district in town,
but I was afraid to go down there.

When I was certain Pastor Gossman was gone, I

walked back outside. The spring night air was invigorating—not really all that chilly. But I was shaking from nervousness about this new venture I had in mind.

I walked a couple of blocks and stood on a corner waiting for some man to come by. I decided I'd charge twenty-five dollars. The whole thing disgusted me, but it seemed to be the only way.

Then I saw him—a man, all by himself, walking toward me. The closer he came, the faster my heart beat. This was a crazy idea. Could I go through with it? I didn't want to. But then neither did I want to starve!

3

The man was about a hundred feet away now and began eyeing me suspiciously. Suppose he was a dirty old man! Suppose he was a pervert! I'd read about teenage prostitutes getting killed by perverts. Now I was really sweating!

But I had to have money. No way was I going to sit around and starve to death! And no way was I going to let my poor dad starve—even if this whole thing was his fault. Mom? Well, maybe all her blubber would keep her alive for a month. A thirty-day fast might be the best thing in the world for her!

When the man got a few steps from me, I moved directly in front of him and blurted out, "Do you want my body for twenty-five dollars?"

The man blinked in surprise. I must have said the wrong thing. Maybe I said it too seriously. I had no idea what prostitutes said or how they acted. Maybe I should have smiled.

So I said it again, this time with my most alluring smile. "Do you want my body for twenty-five dollars?"

The man stepped back and stared at me. I moved toward him, and he started backing up. He threw his hands into the air and said in a disgusted tone, "Now listen here, little girl, I'm not the person for you sorority girls to play your tricks on. Now just move out of the way, and I'll walk on down the street. You can tell your friends about the funny thing you did, but honestly I don't think it's funny for a girl to go up to a man and ask him something like that."

"Hey, mister, this is no joke; I'm serious. I need some money, and I'm willing to do this to get it. It's no trick."

The man put his hands on his hips and said, "Do you know whom you're talking to?"

Oh, no! I'd propositioned a plainclothes cop! Well, how was I to know? He sure didn't look like a cop.

Shaking my head I said, "Sure don't. You a cop?"

"No, I'm a minister. I'm Reverend Berkett, pastor of the United Methodist Church."

I was so chagrined at having propositioned a preacher that without thinking, I blurted out, "That's okay. If you're a preacher, you can have it free."

That really struck his funny bone, and he laughed uproariously. "What's the matter?" he said, trying to regain his composure. "Are you behind on your tithes to the church?"

I laughed, too. He sure was making it easy for me to get out of this embarrassing situation. I appreciated that.

"Young lady, I know this must be a trick," he said. "I can't believe that a beautiful girl like you, with all the potential you must have for life, would be out here on the streets of Kent, selling her body. It just doesn't make sense."

I jumped at the way out he offered me and responded, "Yeah, it was all part of a dare. I was at home reading *The Decline and Fall of the Roman Empire*. It's not my usual reading, you understand, but I get extra credit for reading it for history class. Well, as you know, there was lots of immorality in Rome. My sister saw what I was reading, and we got to talking about prostitution. She dared me to go out and try it. I never was one to back down from a dare, so here I am. And would you believe that the first man I run into is a minister?"

"Well, young lady, maybe it was the Lord who arranged that," the pastor replied. "You might have propositioned someone who would have taken you seriously. This isn't a big city, but there are a lot of sinful people in Kent. For a cute young lady like you to suggest something like this could get you into a lot of trouble. There are perverts looking for girls like you. Even pimps from the big cities come around here. They take girls and make slaves of them. So if I were you, I'd head back home just as fast as I could. You've done a very foolish thing. You ought to stop taking every dare that comes along!"

Being lectured by a minister made me kind of mad, so I snapped, "Hey, preacher, I'll bet you're not so pure and righteous. I noticed you looking me over when you were coming up the street. I'll bet all your thoughts haven't always been pure and holy!"

I stared at him, and he looked the other way. Then he recovered, pointed his finger at me, and ordered, "Young lady, I said for you to get off the street and get home before you get into big trouble!"

No man was going to start ordering me around! "You're the one who'd better get out of here!" I retorted. "Because if you don't, I'm going to go to the police and tell them you came up and propositioned me. I'll tell them you offered me twenty-five dollars. I was just standing here on the corner when you came up to me. Think how that's going to look for you! I know who you are. What are all those little old ladies in your church going to say when they find out what you do at night!"

No sooner were the words out of my mouth than I gasped. Would I really tell lies like that against a minister? What had gotten into me?

The pastor didn't respond to my charges. He just started backing away.

When he finally turned the corner, I stood there prid-

ing myself on how tough I had become. I could handle
people. Why, I had wrapped that minister around my
little finger! Just look at how terrified he was of what I
might do to him. Maybe I should have charged him
twenty-five dollars for not going to the police with that
story!

I stood there on the corner, smiling at the cars that
went by, but nobody stopped. I guessed I'd have to wait
for somebody walking by.

The longer I stood there, the more nervous I became.
Suppose I did proposition the wrong person—like a cop
or a pervert? With my luck I'd probably end up dead.
Oh, well. I'd starve to death if I didn't do this. What difference did it make which way I died?

Up the street I noticed a police car. I moved in the
shadows to a nearby alleyway and pushed up against a
wall. When I heard the car stop, I ducked behind a huge
box.

Were they looking for me? Did that Reverend Berkett
go to the police?

Then I heard his voice saying, "She was just here a
few minutes ago. Maybe she went home like I told her
to."

So that was it! He did go to the police. Smart! Better to
tell them what happened than to wait and see if I told
them!

He was still explaining: "She was a cute little girl, too.
I judged she must be in her early teens although she
tried to look older. I don't know who she was, but she
certainly shouldn't be out in the street doing that kind of
thing. I wish I could have taken her home to my lovely
wife. I really think that girl is starving for love."

I wanted to jump up and say, "Here I am! Can I go
home to someone who'll love me?" I didn't know places
like that existed. That minister sounded sincere.

But was it a trap? Did he say something like that just

to get me out of hiding so that the police would arrest me? After all, the whole situation was my word against his, and he had the cops with him! I crouched lower. No way was I going to be suckered into something like that!

After what seemed like an eternity, I heard car doors slam and the police car drive off. I edged my way back to the street and peered both ways. The coast was clear.

When I turned to the left, I spotted a man leaning up against a building. That frightened me. When he saw me, he called, "Young lady, come here!"

That voice. It was Reverend Berkett. "What are you doing back here?" I demanded.

"Young lady," he said, smiling, "I don't know who you are, but after I left you, I asked the Lord to show me if you were playing games or not. God seemed to speak to my heart and tell me that something terrible was troubling you. That's why I went to the police. I didn't want my reputation ruined by a false accusation, so I had to settle that. I believe God has a lot of things He wants me to do in this community. Well, when I talked to the police, we decided to come back here and see if we could locate you."

"I know," I said. "I heard you talking."

"Yes, and I saw you crouched behind that box," he responded. "I could have called those two officers, and they would have nabbed you. But I didn't feel that having the police take you to jail was the answer. So I told the officers to go back to the station and I'd look for you on my own. So you can thank God that you weren't arrested."

This minister was okay. The more I talked to him, the better I liked him. Maybe I'd go to his church someday.

"Another thing," he went on. "The police tell me they are beginning to crack down on the increasing prostitution in this city. They said they don't know whether it's because of the high unemployment rate here or if women are just doing it for kicks."

"You mean prostitutes are hanging around the streets of Kent?"

"No, not exactly. The police tell me the prostitutes work mainly in the bars. I guess men get drunk and want a woman. These girls know it. But the police are also concerned about how pimps are coming in and taking these girls off to the big cities like New York, Chicago, and Los Angeles."

"I think I'd better go home like you said," I told him. "I think I've heard enough for one night. It was a stupid thing for me to do."

As I turned and started down the street, he stepped beside me. "Young lady," he said, "why don't you come on home with me? I want you to meet my wife. Whatever is troubling you, I know she could help you."

"Oh, come off it, reverend," I replied. "It was just a little prank. I'm okay. I come from a nice family."

"Are you sure?" he asked. "You seem deeply troubled."

I didn't answer, just walked faster. That didn't deter him. He kept pace.

"Listen, come by the parsonage for a cup of hot chocolate. Then you can go home."

I had to shake this guy if I was going to make any money. I didn't have time for somebody to be concerned about me. Maybe if I agreed to come. . . .

"Okay, reverend, I'll come by. But I've got to go tell my folks where I'll be going so they won't worry. I live just two blocks down there." I pointed. "You wait here, and I'll be right back."

"Oh, do you live that close? Great! I'll just walk down there with you to meet your parents. That way I can assure them you're in good company."

This clown was something else! What was it going to take for me to shake him?

"Uh, I don't think that would be too good of an idea," I said. "You see, they're strict Catholics. If they knew I was out at a Protestant minister's house, they'd really be upset. I try to be a little more tolerant myself, but my folks are from the old school. I'm sure you understand."

Of course, I wasn't a Catholic. But I'd heard somewhere that Catholics and Protestants didn't get along. I guess I picked that up from the stories of the civil war in Ireland. Since Reverend Berkett was a Protestant minister, it seemed like the best way to get rid of him.

"Oh, I can't think they'd be upset over your coming by for a cup of hot chocolate," he said. "After all, I'm not trying to convert you. In fact, I'd really like to meet your parents and chat with them. You see, God is doing some great things to bring Protestants and Catholics together. I'm a charismatic Methodist; God has filled me with His Holy Spirit. I've got some wonderful friends who are charismatic Catholics. You know what I'm talking about, don't you?"

I nodded, even though I really didn't quite understand. But I sure didn't want to get into some theological discussion at this hour of the night.

"We charismatics have wonderful fellowship," he went on. "Maybe your parents know some of my Catholic friends—like Father Brynson of St. Mary's here in town. He's charismatic, too. Is that where your family attends?"

Now what was I going to say? I was getting in deeper all the time.

"I guess you might say we're not a churchgoing family," I told him. "I mean, I was born that way, so I call myself a Catholic. But it's been quite a few years since we've been to church."

Reverend Berkett smiled as we got closer and closer to the place I had pointed out as where we lived. "I know what you mean," he said. "I have a few people who are

members of my church but who never come. They have
their names on the church roll and think that will get
them into heaven. But I tell them that's not enough. It
takes a personal relationship with Jesus for a person to
get into heaven. Isn't that right?"

Now he was preaching at me. What could I do to get
rid of him? Should I just tell him the whole truth about
my dad's being an alcoholic and our needing money for
food? Once again I opened my mouth to say it, but the
words just wouldn't come out. My pride, I guess.

I noticed a brightly lit house in the middle of the
block just ahead. He didn't know which house I had
pointed to before. I'd make that house my home. And
I'd get rid of this minister, too.

"Maybe you should talk to my parents about this
charac—"

"Charismatic," he corrected.

"Yes, well, whatever. I always felt guilty about our
not going to church. Maybe you could get us all started
again."

I pointed to the house I had selected. "That's where I
live," I said. "But I don't know what kind of a reaction
you'll get. Let me go ahead and check things out. Okay?
If I can work it out, I'll open the door and motion for
you to come. If I raise my hand straight up, my parents
are angry about the whole idea. Then you'd better wait
until another time."

He smiled. "If you tell them I know Father Brynson,
I'm sure they'll talk to me," he said.

As I opened the gate and walked up the sidewalk to
that house, I was thinking that this had to be one of the
craziest things I had ever done.

When I knocked on the door, a woman answered.
"Hi," I said. "I'm Becky Nelson. I'm having trouble with
my dad's car. We live on the other side of town. Could I
use your telephone to call him?"

they be driving around these streets looking for me? I couldn't take the chance of standing on a street corner now.

I walked several blocks to the middle of town. The only thing open was the pizza place. When I walked by, my stomach took two flips. I loved pizza, and the smell made my mouth water. But I needed money. *Hey, why not rob the pizza place?*

I peered in the window. The guy working had his back to me, and I didn't see anybody else inside. It was a perfect setup. But how could I be sure he wouldn't recognize me? After all, I did come in here for pizza quite often.

I got an idea and headed for a vacant lot a block or so away. An old store there had burned a few months ago. Maybe I'd find there what I needed. If so, then in a few minutes I'd get the money I needed—out of the cash register at the pizza place!

4

The streetlight cast an eerie glow on the vacant lot. I had no trouble at all spotting a stick about six inches long. That was a part of what I needed. Now if I could find a piece of cloth.

Previously I had fussed about how awful it was of the city to let people dump trash on the site of this burned-down building. Now I was glad the cleanup campaign hadn't started yet. That meant I could probably find what I needed to carry out my plan of robbing that pizza place.

I was turning over some of the trash when suddenly a rat screeched and ran toward me from under its hiding place. Terrified, I leaped back. I must have uncovered its nest. I sure wasn't going to argue with it!

I went clear across to the other side of the lot. This time I'd be more careful of rats.

Then I spotted an old sweater buried in the rubbish. Just what I needed! Slowly I pulled it free, hoping not to disturb any more furry rodents!

When the sweater finally jerked free, I balled it up, poked it in my pocket, and ran from that lot as fast as I could.

I still needed a paper bag. I walked into a nearby alleyway, thinking I probably could locate one in the trash. Sure enough, halfway down the alley I saw a bunch of boxes stacked high and started rummaging through them. But I did it cautiously, for I suspected there were rats around here, too.

I stuck my hand into a box and felt a bunch of papers. Probably there were some bags among them. Then it happened! Something was rustling around in those papers! I jerked my hand away and leaped back just as a huge rat sprang from the box!

I took off, and that thing started chasing me! But it gave up the chase quickly when a big black cat appeared out of nowhere and lunged toward it!

Whew! Even though I had run only twenty feet or so, I was completely out of breath. My heart was beating like crazy from the terror of being chased by a rat. I'd heard of people being killed by those huge rats!

I still needed that bag. I hated to go back up that alley. Then it occurred to me that if that cat were around, all the rats would be in hiding. So I cautiously went back to the box, pulled out the papers, and sifted through them to find a bag just the right size. Now I was ready. I headed back to the pizza place, hoping my idea would work.

A few feet from the entrance, in a spot where the guy inside couldn't see me, I started my disguise. I put the bag over my head so I could tell where my eyes would come. I took it off, poked the holes for the eyes, and then put it back on again. I could see out of it a little—not too well. But well enough. Now no one would know me. But I was sure hoping I wouldn't have to run for it; I'd probably trip and fall.

I was just getting ready to get my stick "gun" set when a voice behind me said, "Who goes there?"

I turned and through the holes in the bag saw a man standing there. He threw his hands up in the air in mock horror, yelling, "It's a ghost! It's a ghost!" Then he began quivering as though he were scared to death.

"What's going on?" he demanded. "It isn't time for Halloween; that's in October!"

I was racking my brain for some way to get rid of this clown. "Oh, mister," I said, "you see, I have a little problem. I love pizza, but my mom has me on a diet. To be sure I didn't eat any, she called the guy down here and told him not to sell me any. Well, I'm going to fool them both. I put this bag over my head and he won't recognize me. I mean, I think it's going to be a funny joke on him. But best of all, I'm going to get my pizza!"

The guy laughed. "You kids think of the craziest things," he said. "But you know what? I think it might just work."

"I sure hope so."

"Except for one little problem," he went on.

"Problem? What problem?"

"When you get the pizza, how are you going to eat it? You don't have a hole for your mouth!" He slapped his thighs, laughing uproariously at his own cleverness.

Big deal. Here I was worried about robbing the place, and all this clown could think about was how I was going to eat the pizza.

"Oh, I'll feed myself through the eyes, " I assured him.

"Hey, you got quite a sense of humor," he said. "You ought to be a comedienne."

Not a bad idea. Some comedians make a lot of money. Then I wouldn't be poor anymore. And I could get something to eat without robbing a pizza place!

"Well, good luck," he said. "Do you mind if I stand around and watch what happens? I've never seen a deal like this before."

Did I mind if he stayed around? I didn't need any witnesses watching me rob this place!

"I think I'd better pull this off by myself—no wit-

nesses," I said. "My mother will really get ticked off if
she finds out. I think it might be kind of stupid for you to
be standing around watching. Know what I mean?"

"Hey, I can't see that it'll hurt anything for me to
watch. I'll just stand across the street. The guy won't see
me. I won't tell anybody. Okay?"

It seemed as though every time I tried to do something, somebody wanted to butt in on it. Then I had an
idea.

"Listen, instead of watching from a distance, why
don't we arrange for you to have a ringside seat?" I
asked. "You get a bag and wear it, too. If we both go in
there dressed like this, that pizza guy won't have the
wisp of an idea that he's selling pizza to someone who's
not supposed to have it. He'll just see it's a man and a
woman and think it's some college kids up to a prank."

"Hey, great idea!" the man responded. "I can hardly
wait to tell my wife about this. I mean, this is really
going to be hilarious!"

"Okay, to get a bag, you'll have to go down there
about three blocks." I pointed. "In the third block, just
past that traffic light, is an alley. About halfway up it
you'll see a bunch of big boxes. I found my bag in one of
those boxes."

Actually the alley where I had found the bag was
about a block and a half away. But I had to get this guy
as far away as I could. I'd never robbed before, so I had
no idea how long it would take. But I was sure hoping to
have it over with and be long gone before this clown got
back.

"Gotcha!" he responded. "But I'm going to make my
bag different. I'm going to have one eye and a mouth. I
don't want to have to eat my pizza through the eye!"

We both chuckled, and I knew I had him coming my
way.

"Hurry!" I said. "I'm about to starve on this crazy

diet. And it doesn't help to be here smelling the pizza!"

He spun around and trotted off. I figured I'd have enough time. He wouldn't find any bags where I was sending him.

Just before he got out of sight, he turned and waved. Now was my time.

I put the stick in my right hand, as though I were holding a gun. Then I threw the old sweater over it so the pizza man couldn't tell it was a stick. I adjusted the bag over my head. Ready!

I stepped into the pizza place, and the guy had his back toward me. Without even turning around, he asked, "What do you want on your pizza?"

"Money!" I answered.

He spun around. I pointed the stick draped to look like a gun right at him and in my toughest voice said, "Walk over to that cash register, open it, and give me all your cash. Do what I say, and you won't get hurt."

He threw up his hands and laughed. "Come on; cut the comedy," he shouted. "Take that bag off your head and tell me what you want. I've had enough practical jokers around here tonight."

I jabbed my "gun" toward him and tried to sound mean. "Mister, do what I say, or I'll signal to my husband across the street. He's got a rifle aimed right at your head."

He shuffled toward the cash register, protesting, "You don't have a gun under that sweater. Now tell me what you want."

"Listen, my old man and me are just passing through town, see? The last town we were in a guy tried to get smart, and I had to pull the trigger. I don't want to hurt you, but I'll shoot if you don't hurry!"

This was taking entirely too long. That clown with the paper bag might be back any minute now. I had to sound tougher.

"Did you read in the *New York Times* today on page four about the bag woman who's been knocking off supermarkets? Well, that's me, and now I'm knocking off this pizza place. So move it!"

I was hoping he didn't read the *Times.* I had no idea what was on page four.

"Okay, okay, but don't pull that trigger," he said. "I got a wife and three kids at home, so please don't hurt me."

"All right, but make it quicklike. All I have to do is raise my arm, and my old man starts shooting. We're not afraid to kill!"

He lunged toward the cash register, pushed a button, and the drawer flew open.

"Just the cash," I warned. "If you've got a gun in there, I'm going to let you have it!"

"Listen, lady, I don't have any gun!" the man yelled. "Here! Take the money and get out!"

He shoved a fistful of bills at me. I grabbed them, stuffed them in my pocket, and headed for the front door. But just as I hit the entrance, there stood that clown, and he didn't have a bag.

"Hey, where did you say those bags were?" he asked. "I looked all over and—"

Without answering I dropped my shoulder and hit him square in the stomach. He sprawled backwards, but his flailing arms knocked the bag off my head.

He started yelling; the pizza man started yelling; and I took off, thinking it was probably just as well that I didn't have to stop and take the bag off. At least I could see where I was going now.

I turned at the first corner, ran through an alley, turned again, and then doubled back. I noticed a building under construction and ducked in it to catch my breath.

Within minutes I heard the sirens. I figured they'd never come looking for me in there.

I guess I must have stayed there at least an hour before things seemed calm enough for me to venture out. Now all I had to do was to get home—a little over a mile.

Before I left the safety of that building, I counted my loot—$152. The excitement of having that much money quickly overrode any notions of stopping to buy something to eat. That might be too dangerous. After all, the police might have a description of the clothes I was wearing, and they might be checking in stores for me.

I even decided to take a circuitous route home. So it was longer—at least it avoided the main highway where there likely would be police cars.

It was pretty late when I finally got home. All the lights were out, so I quietly opened the door and tiptoed down the hall to my room. I was so exhausted that I didn't even take off my clothes. I just pulled off my sneakers and snuggled under the covers. It had been a long evening, and I was dead tired. I kept the money in my pocket.

It seemed like I had just gotten to sleep when Mom came in yelling that it was time to get up and go to school. She started right in on me. "Where did you go last night? What time did you get in? I waited up for you. Your father was so drunk that he fell asleep. I put him to bed. Finally I couldn't stay awake, either, so I went to bed."

"Oh, I went over to Sylvia's house," I lied. "Didn't I tell you I was going?"

She looked puzzled.

"Oh, that's right," I went on. "I forgot I left in a huff because of that deal about Dad's spending all our grocery money. Well, Sylvia's been having trouble with math, so I went over to help her. It took a lot longer than I realized to figure out some of those complicated problems. Hope I didn't inconvenience you. Guess I should have called and told you I'd be late. Sorry."

Mom smiled. "Don't tell me you're changing your ways," she said, obviously pleased. "It's about time you got serious about schoolwork. You need a good education if you're going to have a better life than I've had."

Then she added, "Now get up. You're going to be late for school."

I wasn't about to get up while she was in the room and let her see I'd slept in my clothes all night. That would bring another barrage of questions.

"Mom," I lied, "I don't feel very well today. You know, it's my period."

That was one excuse Mom always understood.

"Okay, well go back to sleep. You need the rest."

She left. I was so excited about what I was going to do with that money. But I was also exhausted, and before long I dropped back to sleep.

About noon I awakened, threw off the covers, put on my sneakers, changed my blouse, and walked out to the living room where Mom was watching the soaps on TV. I think she did only two things in life: ate and watched TV.

"How are you feeling?" she asked. Fortunately I had arrived during a commercial. Otherwise she wouldn't even have been aware I was in the room.

"Lousy!" I responded.

"I wish there was something in the house to eat," she said. "That would make you feel better."

As soon as she mentioned food, I realized I was famished. But with $152, buying food was no problem now!

"Maybe if I went out and got some fresh air it would

help," I said. "It's kind of stuffy in here, and I really enjoy getting out on these beautiful spring days. I may even go for a little walk."

Mom didn't respond. I wasn't surprised. The commercial was over while I was talking, and she really hadn't heard what I had said.

The little corner grocery was only two blocks away. I fairly ran to it. Inside I picked up an ice-cream bar, some peanuts, a package of apple turnovers, and a Coke. When I reached into my pocket, pulled out a wad of bills, and whipped off a five, Mrs. Osburn remarked, "Wow, Terri, did you get a job?"

"Yeah, at McDonald's. They held back my pay for the first couple of weeks, so I got a good-sized check today."

Lying was becoming so easy. I had an answer for everybody and everything. Maybe I wasn't such a dumbbell after all. Those grades in school didn't measure everything. They didn't offer a course in lying under pressure.

As soon as I got outside, I crossed the street, sat on the curb, and gorged myself. Who said junk food wasn't good? This was the best!

But when I got through, I thought about Mom and Dad. It really wasn't right for me to gorge and for them to starve. So I headed two more blocks to the supermarket. It wasn't long until I had that cart half full of goodies: steak, frozen vegetables, bread, milk, cereal, lunch meat, eggs, bacon, even a nice big cake.

The groceries came to $48.10. I whipped off two twenties and a ten. It felt so good to have money.

I ended up with four bags of groceries. No way could I carry four bags home, so I asked the cashier if I could borrow a cart if I brought it right back. She said I could.

I guess I was a little surprised. Some of my friends stole these carts from the parking lot. So I really don't know why she trusted me—unless it was obvious to her I couldn't carry four bags by myself.

When I got home, I marched in with one bag. Mom's mouth flew open. I'm not sure if it was from surprise—or in anticipation of having something to eat. Mom's mouth was always flying open!

"What? Where? How?" she sputtered.

"You won't believe this, Mom. I was out walking, and I spotted some money all wadded up—two twenties and a ten. I couldn't believe it. It seemed like something that fell from the sky. I looked around, and there wasn't a soul in sight. Well, the only thing I could think of was you and Dad and how we didn't have anything to eat in the house. So I took the money to the supermarket and bought groceries."

Mom slapped her hands together and yelled, "I just knew something good was going to happen! I just knew something good was going to happen!"

She followed me into the kitchen. "I've got three more bags in the shopping cart!"

Mom went running outside, her fat shaking all over. She hauled in two bags, and I carried in the last one. We put them all on the counter, and Mom started to tear into them to see what goodies I had purchased.

The cake was one of the first things she came to; they had packed it on top. When she found it, all other things came to a halt. She grabbed a knife, cut herself a huge slice of cake, and started stuffing it in. When she saw the disgusted look on my face, she said, "I'm sorry, Terri. I just can't help myself. I knew I was going to die of hunger before the sun went down. Oh, honey, this is absolutely amazing! It's a miracle!"

It was like Christmas. Every time Mom pulled something out of the bag, she'd yell, "Yippee!"

I was too full to eat anything right then, but Mom had another slice of cake. I wondered if there would be any left for Dad when he got home. I knew he'd be starved. But maybe he'd been able to bum a sandwich from someone at work.

I remembered I had told the cashier I'd bring the grocery cart right back. I'd better do that now. We'd left the front door open when we brought in groceries. From the hallway I happened to glance outside and see a police car at the curb. Two cops were getting out. Oh, no! How had they found me this soon?

I spun around and went into the kitchen where Mom was still eating cake. "Mom," I said, "there are two cops coming up our walk. Did Dad do something wrong?"

"Oh, certainly not, honey. He drinks too much, but he'd never do anything wrong. He just doesn't have it in him."

"Mom, I think maybe they're here because I missed school today. Maybe somebody saw me out walking or at the store. They told us at school that they're really going to start clamping down on those who make excuses and stay home from school. They're probably not going to believe why I stayed home. You know how men are about such things. Why don't you just tell them I went to visit my aunt and I'll be back tomorrow."

Would Mom go along with it? I wondered if those cops knew about the pizza robbery. Or were they just following up on our bungled attempt to rob Mrs. Thompson? After all, they did know I was involved in that.

When they knocked on the door, I jumped into a broom closet. My heart was beating wildly.

"Howdy, ma'am," I heard one of them say when Mom went to the door. "Is this the Geiger residence?"

"Yes, it is, officers. I'm Mrs. Geiger."

"We're looking for your daughter, Terri. Is she here?"

I held my breath. Would Mom cover for me? Should I make a break for it? I didn't want to face any cops!

"Oh, I'm so sorry, but Terri went to her aunt's place late last night," Mom said. "Her aunt has been quite ill, and she asked if Terri could come and do a little cooking and cleaning for her. Terri is such a good help around the house. She'll be back tomorrow."

Good old Mom. No wonder I knew how to lie. I'd heard lies from her all my life.

"We need to talk to her," the officer said. "What time will she be home tomorrow?"

"Oh, I'm not positive, but probably around noon."

"As soon as she comes in, could you call me? I'm Officer Hendrickson. Here's my card and phone number."

"What's the matter?" Mom asked. "Why do you need to talk to Terri?"

"I'm really not at liberty to say, ma'am," the officer explained. "But when we talk to her, you have our permission to be there."

"Is my daughter in trouble?" Mom said, pressing the issue. "I mean, has she been a bad girl?"

"As I said, Mrs. Geiger, let's wait until we talk to her tomorrow. Okay?"

"Well, I guess so," Mom said. "But I can't imagine Terri's being in any trouble. My daughter is a very good girl. She's never given us an ounce of trouble. In fact, she looks out for us and for her aunt. My daughter would never do anything wrong. I know that for sure."

After the officers left, Mom came back into the kitchen, and I came out of the broom closet.

She cut herself another big slice of cake. "Terri," she said between gulps, "tell me honestly. Why were those cops here?"

I swallowed hard. "Mom, I don't have the slightest idea. You know I've always been a good girl and tried to do right. Like that money I found today. I could have taken that and bought drugs and gotten high. That's what most of the kids in school would have done. Or I could have gotten drunk. Or even bought myself some new shoes. But, no, what did I do? I bought groceries for our family. Doesn't that prove I'm a good girl?"

"Yeah, honey, I believe you're a good girl. But to-morrow those cops are coming back. I wonder what's on their minds?"

5

I had a pretty good idea of what was on those cops' minds, but I wasn't about to tell my mother. If she knew what I'd done, she'd probably start hitting me the way she knocked Dad around. And if she landed on me, she'd squash me to death!

But I said, "Mom, I have no idea what those cops have on their minds. I mean, I've never done anything in my whole life that would make the cops come to our house. In fact, I'm really embarrassed by this whole thing. I'll bet the neighbors' tongues are already wagging about the cops' being here. No telling what kind of lies they're spreading."

"Yes, I was thinking about that," Mom answered.

"Well, why don't you call the mayor and report those two cops?" I suggested. "It's just awful the way they go around embarrassing honest citizens. Or maybe we ought to call the local paper and get a reporter over here to do an article on these troublemakers. It makes me hopping mad!"

"Now just calm down," Mom told me. "It's probably just a case of mistaken identity. Those cops weren't rude or anything. They're just doing their job."

"What do you mean, they weren't rude? Their showing up here at our house was rude! Very rude! Why didn't they call ahead? Why didn't they send plain-clothes officers in an unmarked car? Here come those big turkeys with guns strapped to their hips, acting like tyrants, looking for a little girl. If I had my way about it, I'd have both of them slapped into jail!"

"Terri! Terri! Calm down," Mom said. "I'm sure it's all a mistake. There's no sense in getting all uptight."

She grabbed the last piece of cake and headed back to the living room and her TV. I went back to my bedroom to think. Those cops would be back tomorrow, and it was no case of mistaken identity. Either they had something on me or they suspected something. What should I do?

I pondered running away. But where could I go? Oh, why did I do something so stupid as to rob that pizza place? Why couldn't I have told those ministers about our family's being out of food?

When Dad came home from work, he couldn't believe all the groceries. Mom told him what I had told her. He didn't ask any questions. Poor man. He said he hadn't eaten anything all day long. And I knew that our having groceries helped relieve the guilt he was suffering for having spent all our food money for liquor.

Mom's love for food had made her into a great cook, and she fixed one of the best suppers I'd ever had. But almost every bit reminded me I had stolen the money for this good food—and that the cops were going to be here to see me tomorrow. I was torn between enjoyment and worry.

We sat around watching TV for a while after supper, but I couldn't get interested in any of the stories. I excused myself and went to my room to plan my course of action for tomorrow. It was only about half-past eight, but I climbed into bed and surprisingly was soon fast asleep.

Then I felt someone shaking me and heard Mom saying, "Terri! Wake up! Wake up!"

"What's the matter?" I asked, rubbing my eyes and

noticing it was still dark outside. "It's not time for school yet, is it?"

"No, it's those two policemen," she said. "They're here with two other men. Dad answered the door and told them you were home. He didn't know about this afternoon!"

I had to come up with a plan right now. No way was I going to face any cops.

"Good grief," I said, "can't they let honest citizens sleep? Well, it's probably mistaken identity, like you said. I guess we might as well get it over with. They're obviously not going to let me get any rest until this is settled. Tell them I'll slip on some clothes and be right there."

Mom patted my shoulder. "I told them again, honey, that you're not a bad girl. I have great faith in you. I'll stick by you."

"Thanks, Mom. I needed that."

She smiled, and I tried to. But my heart was beating wildly. I had to get out of here!

When Mom shut the door, I hurriedly dressed, grabbed my old duffel bag out of the closet, and stuffed it full of clothes. I even stuffed my money into it. Then I opened my bedroom window. I remembered thinking I was glad we didn't live in a two-story house. By going out the window I'd outsmart those cops.

I heaved my duffel bag out first. Then I started to crawl out.

"Young lady, I wouldn't do that if I were you!" a voice below me called.

I jerked my head toward the sound of that voice. Standing a few feet from my window was a cop with his gun aimed in my direction. Without answering him I jumped back inside. I might consider running away, but I sure didn't want to get shot.

That meant I had no choice. I had to go in and face

those two cops. But I decided I would deny everything. I'd come up with a good story, and Mom would confirm it. She'd already lied for me today; she'd do it again.

When I walked into the living room, one of the officers said, "Terri Geiger?"

I nodded mechanically.

"Miss Geiger, we're sorry to disturb you. But I need to have these two gentlemen take a look to see if they can identify you."

The two stepped forward, and I recognized them: the guy who worked at the pizza place and the nut who was going to put the bag over his head and go in with me.

"Is she the one?" the cop asked them.

The two stared at me, studying my features. Then both nodded affirmatively.

With those nods the cop whipped out his handcuffs and started to grab me. "Get your filthy hands off me!" I shouted.

"Now, let's not make this any more difficult than it is," the cop told me. "These two men have identified you as the person who robbed the pizza place last night. I have no choice. We'll have to take you down and book you."

"Mom, tell these louts I was taking care of Aunt Louise last night!" I shouted.

She had her mouth clamped shut. It was the first time I remember seeing my mother when her mouth wasn't moving.

Dad stood there transfixed. I think his mechanical mind was adding up all the pieces. He tried to say something, but no words came out.

"Dad, tell them!" I begged.

"Officer," Dad finally said, stepping up to the spokesman, "I'll swear on my wonderful mother's grave that my daughter was at her Aunt Louise's last night."

Mom gasped.

"See there, officers?" I said. "There's been a terrible mistake!"

"Sorry, young lady, but we have two positive identifications of you. We'll check out your story, but you'll have to come along with us. But first, let me read you your rights."

I listened, but I really didn't hear what he was saying. All the time I was wondering how I was possibly going to get out of this mess. It seemed like a bad dream. Maybe I'd wake up, and. . . .

I wasn't really trying to escape right then, but I must have backed up in such a way that it aroused one of the officer's suspicions. He grabbed me and clamped handcuffs on me. And they hurt just as much as those at Mrs. Thompson's house last night.

"You've made a big mistake!" Dad was still protesting as the officers started to lead me out of the house. "You've got the wrong girl!"

"No, I don't think so," one officer responded. "Mr. Ortho, the owner of the pizza place, thought he recognized Terri when she ran out after the robbery. She had a bag over her head, and it got knocked off, so he saw her face. And this other gentleman, Mr. Caldwell, said he knew the family and thought it was Terri. That's why we had to bring them over to see if they could make a positive identification. I'm afraid, Mr. Geiger, that your little girl has gotten herself into a peck of trouble."

I looked pleadingly at Mom, but she just stood there without saying a word. At least Dad would lie for me.

As the cops led me outside, I noticed some of our neighbors standing on their porches watching. Oh, I was embarrassed. There must be a better way to bust kids like me without arousing the whole neighborhood's gossip. Someday I'd get back at these cops for this humiliation!

With sirens blaring they drove me to the police station. There I was taken to a small room and asked a bunch of questions by a woman officer. They took my picture and fingerprints. Then they searched me and led me to a cell.

As they slammed the cell door behind me, the sound ricocheted down the hallway. And it hit me that this was the beginning of the end for me.

"Hey, what are you in for—prostitution?" a voice asked.

I turned to face a girl about my age, I judged. But did she ever look hard.

"No, it's a case of mistaken identity," I replied. "They think they got me for robbing a pizza place, but I got an airtight alibi. I wasn't near that place last night."

I sure wasn't going to tell her the truth. I'd heard the kids at school who got busted tell how the cops put stool pigeons in the cell with you. You think you're confiding in a friend, and you discover they are there to get the truth out of you and use it against you in court. Well, I wasn't going to trust another cop—especially after they embarrassed me like that in front of our whole neighborhood.

"What have they got you for?" I asked.

"Well, let me see." She started counting on her fingers. "I've robbed banks; I've robbed grocery stores; I've robbed gas stations; I've burglarized homes. You name it, baby, and I've done it. I've even been a prostitute."

I stared at her unbelievingly. She looked awfully young to have been involved in all those things.

"Come on, now," I said. "You haven't really done all that, have you?"

She laughed. "No. They just picked me up for running away from home. I'm from Chicago and was headed for New York City. I was hitchhiking, and some guy took me way out of my way. Then I got picked up by a plainclothes cop. I had identification on me, so they called home. I told them I'd never go back home, so they threw me in here until they can decide what to do with me. But they don't have any real charges against me. I'll be out before long. Jail is no big deal."

I walked over and sat on a bench, eyeing her. Somehow I didn't think she was telling me the truth. Maybe she thought *I* was the stool pigeon!

A matron came to the cell door and asked, "Which one of you is Barbara Hartlin?"

"I'm Barbara Hartlin," the girl said. "What's up, chick?"

The matron bristled. "Don't get smart with me, young lady," she shouted. "You are to address me as Miss Sullivan. Do you understand?"

Barbara laughed. "Hey, don't get so uptight, Sullivan. After all, I could have called you a fat, old hen instead of a chick. You ought to at least give me credit for that."

This Barbara was a smart aleck. I didn't like her attitude. And Miss Sullivan didn't, either.

"Miss Hartlin," she said, "you are slated for an appearance before the judge at ten in the morning. I don't know quite how to tell you this, but we've contacted your mother about appearing in court, and she refused to do it."

Barbara laughed and slapped her thigh. "Hey there, chickie, that's no problem. If Mom showed up, she'd be so drunk that her breath would intoxicate the judge! If he said something she didn't like, she'd spit at him—or throw her whiskey bottle at him. So don't spare me news like that. I'm glad she won't be there!"

The matron wheeled and walked off.

"Wow, that would be a long way for your mom to come from Chicago all the way here to New York State," I said. "Didn't they understand that—"

Barbara's raucous laugh interrupted me. "Terri Geiger, don't you remember me?" she said. "I've seen you at school."

I stared at her. No, I didn't remember her.

"Well, you've probably read about me in the local papers," she said. "I've been busted so many times you wouldn't believe it. They got me for shoplifting, for stealing a car, for possession of drugs. Now they think they've got me for pushing drugs. They say they're going to put me away for good this time."

Drugs? Oh, yes, I did remember this girl. She was the pusher at school. But I stayed away from her crowd. I couldn't see any future in taking drugs.

"I was just giving you a line about Chicago," she went on. "I live here in Kent, too."

"You really think they'll throw the book at you?" I asked.

"Baby, I think I have a way to beat this rap," she replied. "And I hope you do, too. Because if you don't, you'd better hope they don't send you up to Hudsonville. I mean, baby, that training school has got a reputation as the worst in the world. Man, I spent six months there, and during that time at least ten girls got their throats slashed! And that's supposed to be the place for rehabilitating juvenile delinquents!"

I'd never even heard of Hudsonville before. "You don't think they'll send me there, do you?" I asked.

"What's the charge, baby?"

"Well, they say they've got identification that I was the one who robbed the pizza place. I might even be in trouble for trying to knock off Mrs. Thompson's house even though she refused to press charges against me."

"Hey, don't tell me you tried to knock off old lady Thompson?" Barbara asked. "Did you get taken in by that postman's story about her money and jewels? Well,

I found out she's really poor. She doesn't even have enough money to feed all her cats."

"You're kidding! You mean that Thompson deal is a setup?"

"You better believe it. I heard she reads detective magazines all the time and thinks she's the community's answer to a war on crime. Her place is just a big trap, that's all."

I couldn't believe I had been suckered into a thing like that. Why hadn't Sylvia been smart enough to figure it out?

"Why don't the cops put a stop to it?" I asked.

"Are you kidding? That's how the cops catch their quota of robbers. The postman lets the word out. Mrs. Thompson calls the cops. Very simple. If you ask me, it's a good plan to catch crooks."

"Hey, wait a minute!" I protested. "Whose side are you on, anyway?"

"Oh, I can't stand people who would steal from old ladies," Barbara said, looking at me in disgust. "You've just not had any decent upbringing; I can see that."

The more Barbara talked, the more I disliked her. Maybe she'd get sent back to Hudsonville. Hudsonville—was it really as terrible as she'd made it out to be? Certainly the authorities wouldn't let killings go on there, would they? What if I were sent there? Could I survive if it were as bad as she said?

The matron came back and announced I'd be appearing before the judge at ten, also. Then it hit me: What if this Barbara and I were sent together to Hudsonville? I couldn't stand this girl, and it would be just my luck to have to spend a few years in the slammer with her.

Talking with Barbara just made me mad, so when the matron brought some blankets, I laid down and tried to sleep. I closed my eyes, but I don't think I slept a wink that night. It was horrible being in a prison cell. I was frightened, frustrated, angry, bitter—and terribly worried about what lay ahead.

When that eternal night finally ended, they brought us a tray of food—cold, lumpy oatmeal and dry, burnt toast. It tasted horrible, but at this point I really had no appetite anyway.

I was the first one called before the judge. I noticed that Dad was there and another man was with him. He seemed to be a lawyer, but he never talked to me about the case. Dad wasn't drunk, but he'd been hitting the sauce. Where did he get the money for it? Then I remembered. I'd put my money in that duffel bag I'd pushed out the window. Maybe he'd found it. Even the lawyer didn't look like he was totally in control of his senses.

The two of them tried to convince the judge that I had been at my Aunt Louise's house when the robbery occurred. I didn't even have an Aunt Louise, and somehow the judge had found that out! Then Mr. Ortho and Mr. Caldwell identified me as the girl who had robbed the pizza place. If only that stupid bag hadn't been knocked off my head. . . .

Taking a cue from the way Barbara had talked to that matron, I answered the judge rather flippantly a couple of times. Then I realized that was a mistake. He was losing patience with me.

"Miss Geiger," he said, "I understand from this report that you were also caught trying to rob Mrs. Thompson's house that same night. Is that right?"

I stared at the floor. No way was I about to admit to something I wasn't even charged with. The old lady said she wouldn't press charges. What was this dumb judge trying to do to me?

During the deathly silence that followed his question, I knew the judge was staring at me. But I wasn't about to say anything. I had plenty of time.

Then my lawyer nudged me. "You'd better answer the judge, Terri. He's got your life in his hands. So answer him."

I looked the judge right in the eye and said, "Your honor, sir, I don't know what you're talking about."

"Young lady, I'm trying to help you," the judge said in exasperation. "But if you're going to be uncooperative and belligerent, I might have to send you to a place where they can straighten you out."

Threats. Just threats. I was too young for Hudsonville. Besides, it was my first offense. He'd slap my wrists and let me go home. I just knew it. So no way was I going to confess to another crime. If they had me for two burglaries, he might send me away.

"Young lady, how do you plead to the charge of robbing Ortho's Pizza Place?"

I stared at the floor again. Why should I admit anything?

The judge thundered it again: "Young lady, I'm losing my patience with you. How do you plead?"

Dad mumbled, "You'd better answer him, Terri."

I was scared to death. I knew they had me. Maybe if I pleaded guilty, they'd feel sorry for me and let me off.

"Guilty, your honor."

"That's better," the judge responded, settling back in his chair. "Because you have pleaded guilty, I'm going to sentence you to only one year."

I jerked my head up. What did he say? *Only* a year? A year seemed like an eternity!

He slammed down his gavel and said, "I hereby sentence Miss Terri Geiger to one year at the State Training School at Hudsonville."

I gasped. Hudsonville? That's where they slashed girls' throats! I couldn't live in a place like that!

"Your honor," I screamed, "please give me another

chance. I've never done anything like this before. Don't you understand? I've got a drunken father. My mother is a junk-food junkie and lives only to eat and watch TV. I don't have a chance in this life. Can't you show me some mercy?"

I was standing up, shouting at the judge, and two policemen grabbed both of my arms and held me. "Young lady, I know what you're trying to say," the judge told me. "I know about your home. It's all here in this report." He raised a sheaf of papers. "I wish all young ladies came from good homes, but you don't. Sending you home isn't going to solve anything. I have no recourse but to send you to Hudsonville. It has to be that way."

All the fight drained out of me as the cops led me back to my cell. But when I got back there, I began to cry. My world had come to an end.

Maybe this was all a bad dream. Maybe I didn't go with Sylvia to rob Mrs. Thompson's place. Maybe I hadn't pulled that caper at the pizza place. In anger and frustration I went over and kicked the cell door. It was very real. This was no dream.

An hour or so later a matron came and explained to me where I was going.

"Why didn't they send me to a foster home?" I asked. "Why didn't they give me a chance? I'm no criminal."

"That's what they all say," the woman sneered. "You should have thought about all this before you robbed that place."

Oh, she was coldhearted! It made me so mad that I yelled, "Okay, bright eyes, I don't need any preaching from you. I was just asking for a little sympathy and understanding. Obviously you have no idea what those are!"

She bristled. "Don't you get smart with me," she snapped. "I've had to deal with smart ones, and you sound just like all the others. Big mouth—and no brains!"

I clenched my fist, determined to paste her one right in her fat mouth. But when I threw my fist forward, she grabbed my arm and spun me around. The next thing I knew I was flat on the floor and she was glaring down at me.

"You little brat!" she screamed. "I ought to slap you silly. Next time you take on somebody, you'd better find out if they've had karate lessons! I teach karate, so I can handle punks like you."

She had me this time, but. . . .

"You're lucky you're a juvenile," she yelled. "By law I can't lay a hand on you except to protect myself. If you were just a little bit older, I would have kicked you black and blue. Now get up off that floor before I do it anyway!"

I slowly got up, rubbing my back and shoulder. That concrete floor sure was hard.

She grabbed up all her papers and stalked out of the cell in a huff. I yelled after her, "Next time you come in here, I'm going to be ready for you, you beast!"

She wheeled around, pushed my cell door open, and yelled, "Listen, you filthy little brat, I'll be ready for you. I hope you do try something. It'll give me an excuse to really tear into you—in self-defense, of course."

Her sarcasm was driving me up the wall. "I'm going to learn karate, too," I hissed, "and if I ever run into you again, you're going to be the one down there on the floor!"

She slammed the door and walked off. Suddenly I felt vicious and tough. I wondered if this was how all prisoners felt. In fact, I was so mad that if I had had a knife, I wouldn't have hesitated to slash her throat. And I wasn't even in Hudsonville yet!

A few minutes later they brought Barbara back to the

cell to get her things. "I beat the rap," she whispered to me. "The guy I was supposed to have sold drugs to—he never showed up to testify against me. Of course, I warned that dude that if he opened his mouth, I'd have my big brother kill him. Baby, it's like I told you, I beat it!"

Suddenly the whole system seemed terribly wrong. Here was Barbara, a repeat offender, charged with pushing drugs, a horrible crime. And she was getting off scot-free. And here I was, a first-time offender, guilty of taking $152 from a pizza place, using a stick for a gun, and getting a year at Hudsonville. It just wasn't fair.

"I heard what the judge did to you," Barbara said. "Baby, I worry about someone as naive as you going up to Hudsonville. You keep your eyes and ears open up there; do you hear? When you get there, let people think you're the toughest dude around. Don't let anybody push you around. And watch out for the lesbians! Put up a big front; make sure they're scared of you. Otherwise, you've really got problems!"

The guard told Barbara to hurry and get out. I stood watching her go and wondering what was ahead for me. I wasn't the kind of person she was saying I needed to be up there. I couldn't cut anybody's throat. Or could I? I did know I was scared to death.

Two men stopped at my cell a few minutes later and unlocked it.

"Now what?" I asked

"Hudsonville, next stop," one of them said jokingly. I didn't think it was at all funny.

I don't know why, but instinctively I raised my hand to my throat. It must have been overwhelming fear. Was it a prophecy of what was ahead for me?

Would I ever come out of Hudsonville Training School alive?

6

I had no idea of where Hudsonville was, but as we drove there that afternoon, it seemed like it must be on the other side of the world. Maybe it was because I was so scared that the trip seemed so long.

I discovered the place was way out in the country—I mean, way out on a lonely, almost deserted road.

When we arrived, some guards opened a gate in a high fence. Then we drove some more to the main institution. More guards, more fences. I realized one thing: It sure was going to be hard to break out of here!

As the two officers led me to the reception area, I noticed a huge girl leaning up against a wall, a cigarette hanging out of her mouth. She wore a sick green, ill-fitting dress. As we passed her, she snarled, "Do what they say, kid, or you're in for big trouble."

Was she friend or foe? She didn't look like someone I'd want for a friend—big, ugly, fat. And she was probably quick with a knife.

The two officers who brought me signed me in and left me with some woman who took me to her office. She had a whole sheaf of forms—seemed like a hundred pages—for me to go through. I had to give her all kinds of histories—about my family, about my feelings, about why I had robbed the pizza place. Half the answers I gave were lies, but the woman didn't seem to know or care. It was just a routine she had to do.

When we finally got through all the forms, she said she was taking me to the hospital.

"Hospital?" I asked in surprise. "This place doesn't look like a hospital."

She gave me a kind of funny smile and said, "This place is whatever you make it. Some people make it the worst penal institution in the world. Others make it a country resort. And you, Miss Geiger, can make it what you want to make it. I just meant that as far as I'm concerned, this is a hospital."

"And I suppose you're a nurse!" I snapped.

"Okay," she said, "we're getting started on the wrong foot. I want you to know I won't stand for your sarcasm. I have ways of handling it. Now my name is Miss Kirk. Before you open your mouth to me again, you start off by saying 'Miss Kirk.' Is that clear?"

First it was that ugly beast in the reception area; now it was this ugly beast. I knew I was going to hate this place. So help me, first chance I got, I was bailing out.

"Miss Geiger, let me level with you about this place," Miss Kirk went on. "Obey the rules and have respect for those of us in authority, and you'll have your sentence shortened. Disobey the rules and act snotty, and you'll do your full time plus. The judge sentenced you to a year up here. We have ways of getting that time extended if you aren't being rehabilitated. It's up to you."

I didn't feel like listening to a lecture. My head was spinning just from the idea of having to adjust to prison so quickly. But I had enough sense to clamp my mouth shut. I was beginning to realize that the system had tremendous power over me.

Miss Kirk stood up and announced, "Come with me, Miss Geiger. I'll show you to your hospital room."

Hey, maybe this wasn't going to be so bad after all. I could just lay in bed, and they'd bring me my meals!

We left the reception/administration building and

walked along a sidewalk to another building. It was dusk, but I noticed that everything was green: green uniforms, green buildings, green grass, green trees. Even the sky looked green. And it wasn't a pretty green—at least not the buildings and the uniforms. It reminded me of pea soup, and that had never been one of my favorite foods.

Once inside the building Miss Kirk led me to a room filled with showers. "Take off all your clothes and shower," she ordered.

She stood there, arms folded across her chest, watching as I undressed. I felt so embarrassed. I turned toward the wall, but I really wanted to wrap my bra around her neck and choke her to death. Couldn't she give me the decency of some privacy?

As I turned on the shower, she tossed me a bottle and said, "Rub that into your hair. And I mean thoroughly."

I looked at the bottle quizzically, then opened it and smelled it. The orange-colored liquid didn't smell like any shampoo I had ever used. "What in the world is it?" I asked.

"It's for lice," she said matter-of-factly.

"Lice?" I screamed. "I don't have lice. I don't have fleas. I don't have VD. I don't have bugs. I may not be the best girl in the world, but I keep myself clean."

I tried to hand the bottle back to her, but she shoved it into my face. "Miss Geiger, you are going to wash yourself with this. Do you understand? Every square inch of your hair. Sometimes we get a girl in here with lice. When that happens, everybody has lice. Now I don't care whether you have them or not, you're going to scrub your hair thoroughly with this. And wash every part of your body like you've never washed before. Is that clear?"

When I protested that this was ridiculous, that I didn't have any lice, she grabbed me and spun me around, her arms around my throat. "Either you wash yourself with this and kill all those lice, or I'm going to force open your mouth and cram this bottle down your throat. One way or another we're going to get rid of those lice. Now don't make it tough for yourself!"

She grabbed my arm and started twisting until the pain was more than I could stand. "Okay! Okay! I'll wash with your stupid stuff," I yelled. "Just let go of my arm!"

She released me, and I turned toward her as I backed off. Her eyes glanced up and down my naked body, and I shuddered at the way she looked at me.

I knew one thing for sure. I'd never trust this Miss Kirk.

I grabbed the bottle and headed for the shower. Miss Kirk watched every move I made. There were no curtains on the shower. One of the things I was learning about prison life was that I had absolutely no privacy. I'd always had my own room at home. Now I couldn't even take a shower without being watched!

Well, I washed myself thoroughly with that disgusting disinfectant. The odor stayed on my body for weeks.

When Miss Kirk was satisfied that I had washed thoroughly enough, she ordered me out of the shower and threw me a towel. She continued to watch my every movement as I dried. When I started to pick up my jeans, she snapped them out of my hands. "That's the last time you'll see those jeans!" she announced.

I grabbed them back, yelling, "I've always worn jeans. There's no lice in them. Come on!"

She pulled. I pulled. And she yelled, "Miss Geiger, let go this minute!"

I didn't. I pulled harder and caught her off balance. She came toward me, and suddenly I realized she wasn't holding the jeans at all. Her hands grabbed my hair and started twisting. "Listen, you little brat," she yelled, "you haven't been here two hours yet, and already you've given me more trouble than some of these girls do the whole time they're here. Now if you don't straighten up this minute, it's going to be bad for you. And I mean, *really* bad!"

I dropped the jeans at her feet. I guess it was silly to fight over something so trivial.

But what was I going to wear? Certainly she wouldn't make me run around in my underclothes.

My unasked question was quickly answered as she threw a beat-up green gown toward me.

"What's this?" I asked.

She got that funny little smile again. So help me, someday I would slap her face silly.

"It's your uniform. Put it on."

I opened it. Inside I noticed the word *hospital* written on the back.

"Hospital?" I asked.

She said nothing as I slipped the gown on. Then she commanded, "Follow me!"

She led me down a hall. As we passed several girls, I mumbled hello, but they didn't respond. They looked sedated, like walking zombies. Were they all on tranquilizers to keep them calm?

But they all kind of bowed toward Miss Kirk. She seemed like a dictator with a bunch of slaves!

We turned a corner and went about halfway down another hallway to a place where there apparently were a lot of small rooms—at least there were a lot of doors. There was no way to see what was behind those doors; they were solid metal.

Finally Miss Kirk stopped, unlocked and opened one of those doors, and ordered me, "Get in."

The room was just a little bigger than a bathroom— big enough for a cot, a sink, and a toilet. This was a hospital room?

"Could I be on a ward with other people?" I asked. "I really don't need a private room."

Miss Kirk, without a word, pushed me into the room and slammed the door behind me. Then I heard a *click*.

Caught off balance, I sailed across the little room and hit the other side. When I spun around, I was in for a shock. The door had no handle inside. There was no way I could get out. My comings and goings totally depended on someone else!

Up above was a naked light bulb. By the dimness of its light, I figured it couldn't have been more than forty watts.

Noticing a small slit in the door, I went over, stood on tiptoe, and looked out into the hall. I couldn't see far, but in that distance there was no one in sight.

The room had no windows—only that little slit in the door. I knew now it was evening. But how could I tell when it was morning?

I sat on the hard bed, surveying my new home. Then I heard footsteps in the hall. I dashed to the door and stood on tiptoe again so I could see out. When whomever it was got near my door, I called, "Hey, can I ask you a question?"

A face came up next to mine, and a girl said, "What's the matter with you?"

"I don't know who you are, and you don't know me," I said. "But I'm new here. Is this a prison or a hospital?"

The girl stepped back and began to shriek like a hyena. It was sadistic! "What's the matter, girl? Don't you know where you are?"

"No. Where am I?"

"You're in Hudsonville, baby. Hudsonville."

"I know that," I answered. "But I thought I was being sent to a prison. Miss Kirk said it was a hospital. Have they sent me to a mental institution?"

The girl shrieked again, and the sound of it made me

almost certain that they had sent me to a place for crazy people. Maybe I'd gone crazy. Maybe that's why I robbed that pizza place. After all, what I had done and why I had done it might not have made too much sense to the authorities.

The girl walked back to the little slit in the door, her eyes lined up exactly with mine. That look terrified me. Then she whispered, "Look, I don't know who you are or why you're here, but you're in solitary confinement!"

"Solitary confinement? You sure?"

"Yes, baby, I'm sure."

"But my gown says *hospital*. Where's the hospital?"

She gave another sick laugh as she responded, "Baby, there ain't no hospital. They just put that on you new girls to calm you down. This ain't no hospital. This is a prison, and you're in solitary." She laughed again.

I watched her walk away, then I slowly turned to face my new home again. So it wasn't a hospital. They had put me in solitary confinement. But why? I hadn't been here before. I hadn't caused a disturbance among the other girls. I didn't even know any other girls here.

It didn't make any sense that I would be in solitary confinement. They kept that for incorrigible prisoners. Then it dawned on me that this must be a mental hospital. Or was it a prison? My head was spinning. Was I crazy? Or were they trying to make me go out of my mind?

I sat on the bed and stared at the floor—then at the ceiling, then the walls, then the toilet and the sink. This had to be a bad dream.

In anger and frustration I went over and started beating on the wall. My hands hurt, and the reality of my dilemma slowly sifted into my befuddled brain. This wasn't a dream. It was a real-life drama. I was a prisoner either in a prison or a mental hospital. I didn't know which. But I was very much a prisoner.

Then everything broke loose inside me and I threw myself on the bed and sobbed hysterically. Didn't anyone care about me? And if this were solitary confinement, why did they put me in here? I wasn't that bad. Stealing $152 from a pizza place wasn't exactly the greatest crime of all time!

I cried and sobbed and sobbed and cried for a long time. Finally I just lay there, exhausted. What was going to become of me now? I sure didn't know.

Then I heard some footsteps and something rattling on the floor. I looked toward my door and saw a tray of food being pushed under it. They wouldn't even let me out to eat my meals!

I jumped off the bed and, pulling the tray out of the way, got down on my hands and knees to try to see out the hole where the tray had been pushed through. All I saw was two feet.

"Hey, out there, bend down and talk to me!" I called.

The girl who had brought the tray bent down, her face on the floor. She smiled—the first smile I had seen since I'd been here.

"What's your name?" I asked, returning her smile.

"Piggy."

"Piggy? I'm Terri Geiger. Can I ask you a question?"

"Make it quick, girl. I'm not supposed to talk to the prisoners. I can get in big trouble for this."

"Tell me where I am."

"You're in Hudsonville Training Center, and you're in solitary confinement."

"Is this a hospital? Like maybe a mental hospital?"

"No, they just make you think that. You're really in solitary confinement."

"But why solitary confinement?"

"Did you act kind of smart to Miss Kirk?" Piggy asked.

"Yes, I guess so. But she deserved it. She's really a pain."

Piggy laughed. "Then that's why you're here. Miss Kirk is a. . . . I mean, I really can't say enough bad things about her. But I can tell you this. Whenever a new girl comes in and starts acting a little smart, Miss Kirk slams her into solitary. I know. That's what happened to me."

"But isn't that pretty extreme?"

"Terri, you have to get used to the system here. The first thing they do is make you afraid of them. After all, their lives are at stake every time they come among us. There are more of us than them, you know. So they use scare tactics—like Miss Kirk's putting you in solitary to wear down your resistance. After you've been in there for a while, you'll be willing to do whatever she says to get out. She calls it breaking down barriers. Once the barriers are broken, you'll do whatever she says. And I mean *anything!*"

"Are you a prisoner, or do you work here?" I asked.

"No, I'm a prisoner. But I've learned to adjust to the system, and they give me some pretty good jobs. You know, like serving meals to the people in this section. This is an easy job. But I've been here five years."

"Five years?" I asked incredulously.

"Yes, I came when I was eleven. But in nine more months I come up before the review board again. Maybe I'll get out this time."

She jumped up, saying, "I have to be going, Terri. I had to bring you a late tray because you came in late, you know. And they'll be on my case if I'm down here too long. I'll see you in the morning. In the meantime, just stay cool, man. Just stay cool. Don't hassle Miss Kirk, and you'll be out of there in a few days."

With that she was gone.

I picked up the tray and carried it over to my bed.
There wasn't even a table to put it on.

We had stopped for a snack on the way up, so I wasn't
all that hungry. But the sight of the food on this tray
made me want to vomit. It sure smelled horrible. I guess
that was the cabbage. It was all shriveled up and smelled
spoiled. And the hot dog looked as though it was left
over from the World Series of 1932. And there was a
piece of dry, hard bread.

I searched around the tray for some silverware—
nothing, not even a napkin. They expected me to eat this
slop with my fingers!

The whole idea so revolted me and the food so nau-
seated me that I decided I'd show them. I wouldn't eat! I
put the tray down on the floor. But that nasty cabbage
was stinking up my cell. It smelled even worse than that
disinfectant. So I took the tray and shoved it through
that slot under the door out into the hallway.

About an hour later I heard someone pick up the tray,
but by the time I got to the door, whomever it was had
gone.

Once again I flopped onto the bed, turned onto my
back, and stared at the ceiling. Not only was it dirty, but
the corners were filled with cobwebs. Cobwebs! That
meant I was sharing this cell with spiders! I shuddered.

The room had a musty, damp smell to it. I knew if I
didn't get out of here soon, I'd either go crazy or kill
myself. I couldn't live like this.

It was useless to try to sleep. Too many thoughts and
fears flitted in and out of my mind.

Then I heard someone in the hall, rattling keys this
time. It sounded like a key going into my door! Maybe
someone was coming to let me out. At least whomever it
was wouldn't find me crying and screaming. I'd already
gotten that out of my system.

The door creaked open, and there stood Miss Kirk.

She looked so enormous. She must have been close to six feet tall, and she was heavy. She wasn't flabby fat like my mother; she was solid.

"I understand you didn't eat your supper!" she thundered. "Is that right?"

What was wrong with not eating supper? Was that a violation of the rules? Remembering what Piggy said about obeying the rules, I figured I'd better not get smart with her. I wanted to get out of solitary.

"Miss Kirk, I just wasn't hungry," I said. "The two officers stopped for a snack on the way up here, and—"

"I don't care whether you were hungry or not!" she interrupted. "The next time we bring you something to eat, we expect you to eat it. I don't care if you like it or not. You are to eat everything we bring you. Every bit of it. Do you understand?"

"Yes, ma'am," I said respectfully. It almost killed me to be civil to her, but I sure wanted to get out of solitary. Maybe she would think I had learned my lesson and let me out now.

"Here, take this," she ordered, thrusting a box toward me.

"I'll be sure to eat all of it, Miss Kirk," I replied.

She grunted. "It's not food. I guess I should go back to the kitchen and get your tray and stand here while you finish everything on it. You see, we get smart people in here who try to rebel by not eating. They think they are going to starve to death and create problems for the administration. Well let me tell you, Miss Geiger, that if you have ideas like that, you can forget them. We're not about to let anybody starve here. If you don't eat everything on your tray, I or one of my assistants will come in and cram every crumb down your throat. Is that clear?"

I nodded. Whatever Miss Kirk said, I knew I was going to have to do. I had no choice. I guess that's one of the things about losing your freedom in prison.

"In that box is a puzzle," she went on. "If you can put that puzzle together, I'll let you out of this cell."

At last there was hope!

Miss Kirk put a key in the door to let herself out and slammed the door behind her. I heard more rattling of keys and knew she was locking me in.

Over on my bed, I opened the box. There must have been a thousand tiny pieces in that box. Puzzles were never my thing, but if putting a puzzle together was what it took to get out of solitary, then I'd put a puzzle together.

I dumped the pieces onto the floor, got down on my hands and knees, and started in. I kid you not when I say I spent that whole night working on that stupid puzzle. It was one of the most exhausting, mind-blowing experiences I have ever had! I kept fighting sleep. I would slap my face to stay awake. Then I'd douse it with cold water.

My knees ached from kneeling on that cold concrete floor. My back ached from bending over. No way could I get comfortable as I worked feverishly. But no matter what it took, I was determined to finish that puzzle!

I was almost finished—just three more pieces. But where were they?

I scoured the floor for them. Why had I dumped them out so carelessly? I shook my blanket. I even looked under the mattress. I took off my gown and shook it. I pushed my hand underneath the door and into the hall. I had to find those three pieces.

After I had exhausted every means, I just knew those three pieces couldn't possibly be anywhere in my cell. I was so tired I couldn't see straight. I flopped onto my bed and fell into a troubled sleep.

A rattling of keys in the door awakened me. I jumped out of bed just as Miss Kirk entered my cell.

"Miss Kirk, I've finished the puzzle," I said, pointing with pride at my accomplishment.

"My, you've been busy, haven't you?" she said. "I'll bet you hardly slept a wink all night." Then she looked closer. "What's this? There seem to be some pieces missing. Let's see: one there, and one there. My, there are three pieces missing. I knew you were a thief, but I didn't think you'd steal three pieces of my puzzle." Her words dripped with sarcasm.

"I didn't steal them, Miss Kirk. Why would I steal them? They just weren't in the box."

"Oh, but they were," she responded. "All the pieces were in the box when I handed it to you. I know positively that not one of those pieces was missing. Now what did you do with them?"

"Miss Kirk, so help me, I have spent hours looking for those missing pieces," I said, trying to choke back the tears. "I have looked in every conceivable place. I swear they are not here. They had to have been missing from that box."

"Are you calling me a liar, Miss Geiger? I know my puzzles. I know the prisoners here. And I know for certain all the pieces were in that box when I handed it to you. I sure don't know what you're trying to pull."

As she backed to the door, I yelled, "But, Miss Kirk, you said I could get out of solitary when I finished the puzzle. That's what you said."

"Of course I said that," she soothed. "But as I recall, I said you could get out when you had *finished* the puzzle. A puzzle with three pieces missing is hardly finished!"

She slammed the door behind her. I ran against it, but it didn't budge. All it did was hurt my shoulder.

"As soon as you put those last three pieces in the puzzle, you can get out, Miss Geiger," she called from the hallway.

"But how can I finish it if I can't find the pieces?" I shouted back.

"I think that's your problem, not mine," she responded. Then I heard her footsteps going away.

Frantically I yanked everything off my bed and shook it wildly. No pieces. I ran my hands over every square inch of that floor. I looked in the sink—even in the toilet. Those three pieces could not possibly be anywhere in this cell. But where were they?

Then I heard something rattle underneath the door— the breakfast tray.

"Is that you, Piggy?" I called.

"Yes. Sorry I'm late. Miss Kirk made me wait until after she had been down here this morning."

"Yes, she came down here with a puzzle last night and said I could get out if I finished it," I said. "I worked on it all night, but there are three pieces missing."

Piggy laughed.

"What's so funny?"

"Did you say three pieces were missing?"

"Yes."

"And has Miss Kirk been here and told you she was positive all the pieces were in the box when she gave it to you?"

"Yes."

"And that you can't get out until you find those three pieces?"

"Hey, how did you know? Did she tell you about our conversation?" I asked.

"No," Piggy responded. "I'm sorry. I should have warned you last night when I brought your supper tray."

"Warned me? About what?"

"Push your face down here close to this opening," Piggy told me. "Miss Kirk would kill me if she found out I told you this. Terri, you'll never find those three pieces. She kept them out deliberately!"

"What?" I yelled. "What did you say?"

"Terri, shush, for crying out loud, or we'll both be in deep trouble. She'd throw me in solitary, and you'd be a longer time getting out. Now what I said was that Miss Kirk deliberately kept out three pieces of that puzzle."

"But why?"

"Terri, you'll have to get used to the system. She gave you that puzzle to shut you up last night. That's the whole name of the game—keep the prisoners quiet so they don't cause an uproar. She knew you'd be up all night working on it. That was to keep you quiet. Her keeping the three pieces out is to break you. She gave you hope by telling you that you could get out if you finished the puzzle. But now you find out there is no possible way you can finish it. You're still going to have to do what she says to get out."

"But what am I going to do?" I wailed. "Can you sneak those missing pieces in on my lunch tray?"

"You think I'm crazy?" Piggy responded. "I've got nothing to gain and everything to lose for something stupid like that. Besides, I don't know where she keeps her puzzles. She plays this trick on all the new girls."

"But when am I going to get out of here?"

"When Miss Kirk comes back, just stay cool, man, and do whatever she says. You have to play the game according to her rules, you know. Don't rebel or act smart. Don't yell back. Just stay cool."

"Okay, Piggy, I'll try. And thanks!"

"Don't mention it. I have to split." And she was gone.

I grabbed the breakfast tray and for the first time realized it was oatmeal. I hardly ever ate breakfast at home, and I wouldn't be caught dead eating oatmeal. But now I had to eat every bite of it or face the wrath of Miss Kirk.

No spoon. No sugar. No milk. I started to dip some out with my fingers. Ugh. It was ice-cold!

I was like a baby trying to eat with my fingers. I got that nasty stuff all over my mouth. Some of it dropped onto my gown. And it almost gagged me as I tried to swallow it. Cold, lumpy oatmeal—never in my wildest nightmares had I thought I would ever be subjected to something like this!

I finally got it all down, even though my stomach complained the whole time. I felt like some savage in the jungle, totally uncivilized.

Miss Kirk was somehow behind everything that happened, it seemed. Oh, how I hated that woman! I knew she'd be back again to torment me. Somehow, some way, I ought to kill that woman. I'd be doing this whole place a favor to get rid of her.

I pushed the empty tray through the slot at the bottom of the door and lay back down on my bed. I didn't know for sure what I was going to do, but when she opened that door again, I wasn't just going to sit here and take all that guff from her!

7

It wasn't long after breakfast that I heard the keys rattle, and the door opened. There stood Miss Kirk, smiling that fiendish smile of hers.

"Well, I noticed you finished your breakfast like a good girl," she started in. "And have you finished the puzzle?"

"I sure did," I responded.

She looked down at it. "Oh, I don't think so," she replied. "It looks to me like there are three pieces missing."

I glared at her. I knew she had those pieces, but I couldn't tell her I knew without getting Piggy in trouble.

"Here's something to help you pass the time in here," she said. From behind her back she extended three books toward me.

I kept my hands at my side and blurted out, "Now just a minute, Miss Kirk. Let's discuss the puzzle first. We had a deal. You said that if I finished the puzzle, I would get out of solitary. Well, I finished the puzzle."

"Oh, I distinctly remember saying the word *finished*," Miss Kirk said in a sickeningly sweet tone. "And I don't call a puzzle with three pieces missing finished. Look." She pointed at the floor.

I didn't even glance down.

"I think I remember telling you before breakfast that

unless you found those three pieces, the puzzle wasn't finished. Don't you remember that?"

Her attitude was driving me up the wall. I clenched and unclenched my fist. Did I dare hit her? If I did, it would have to be hard enough to knock her out because I knew I'd really have to pay for it. I never was much of a fighter. She'd probably have me on the floor in a minute—just like that karate instructor back in Kent.

She still extended the books toward me, but I was too furious to talk about books. "Miss Kirk," I said as deliberately as I could, "you have those three pieces, don't you?"

"Whatever are you talking about?" she asked in feigned surprise.

"So help me, Miss Kirk, I have scoured every inch of this cell for those missing pieces. I believe you kept them out on purpose just to frustrate me, maybe to make me do something violent so you'd have a reason to keep me in solitary longer."

"My, we have a suspicious nature, don't we?" she said in that sweet tone. I knew she was toying with me. "But let me tell you something, Miss Geiger. Last week another new girl had that same puzzle and put it together. I mean, every single piece. After we released her from solitary, I personally picked up the pieces and put them in that box. I made certain I'd put in all the pieces. I wouldn't want to do anything to frustrate you new girls, such as giving you an impossible task. So I know all those pieces were in that box when I gave it to you last night. Since you can't find them, I guess that. . . ."

She never did finish the sentence. I was so angered and frustrated by her lies that I jumped on the puzzle and kicked it until the little pieces scattered in every direction. Then I spit on it, saying, "That's what I think of your stupid puzzle!"

I expected Miss Kirk to jump on me. But she just stood there grinning and repeating, "Temper, temper, temper!"

That did it. I started screaming and jumping up and down on the pieces.

This time she did grab me, yelling, "Calm down, young lady. Here. Take these books." She extended them again. I clenched my fist and came down hard on those books. They flew out of her hand and hit the floor. And right by them I saw three pieces of the puzzle. They had to be those three missing pieces.

I was choking back tears of frustration and anger as I knelt down and tenderly picked up those three pieces. When I looked up at her, she said, "I told you I didn't have those three pieces. If you had read these books as I told you to, you would have found the pieces in one of them. Then you could have finished the puzzle and gotten out. Now I don't know whether you'll ever find all the pieces or not. But let me tell you, Miss Geiger, that you're not getting out of solitary until you put every piece in that puzzle!"

She spun around and left me with a thousand pieces of puzzle scattered all over that cell and a million thoughts racing through my mind. Enraged, I got up and kicked the cell door—hard. It didn't budge, but my foot sure hurt. I was going to have to remember to take out my frustrations some other way. So far, all I was doing was hurting myself.

I looked at all those pieces. If I did finally succeed in getting that whole thing together again, would she really let me out? Or would she have some other trick up her sleeve? I knew I could never trust her. But so help me, she wasn't going to get the best of me. Someday I'd get even!

With tears in my eyes, I bent over and started the la-

borious task of putting that puzzle back together. I had
no choice. I had to go this route to see if Miss Kirk
would keep her promise.

Fortunately my temper tantrum hadn't separated
every piece. That was one time I was thankful for inter-
locking puzzles. It meant a little less time and effort for
me.

I was just about to finish the border when someone
slipped a lunch tray under my door.

"Hey, Piggy," I called, bending down by the opening,
"is that you?"

A face looked back at me. Sure enough, it was Piggy.

"Hey, Piggy, you know what? That fat slob, Miss
Kirk, had those missing pieces!"

No sooner were the words *fat slob* out of my mouth
than I knew I'd made a big mistake. I had realized from
the size of Piggy's feet and the fatness of her cheeks that
she had to be pretty hefty herself. And I was right.
Without a word she got up and was gone. I knew I'd
better never mention *fat* to her again!

I ate the sandwich and drank the soup from the bowl
and went back to work on the puzzle. I was waiting for
supper, hoping somehow I could straighten things out
with Piggy. So far she was my only help.

When the supper tray was pushed under my door, I
bent down again, and said, "Hey, Piggy, is that you?"

She grunted.

"I'm sorry about this afternoon. I apologize."

Her smiling face appeared on the floor, looking in at
me.

"Miss Kirk had those three missing pieces," I said.
"What do you think of that?"

She smiled back at me. "That's what that big old fat
slob will do to you," she responded. "She gets her kicks
trying to drive us crazy. But don't let her get to you,
Terri."

So Piggy called her a fat slob, too. Maybe there was some other reason she took off so fast this noon. But I sure wasn't taking any chances; I wasn't going to refer to fat around Piggy again.

"You think she'll pull more tricks?" I asked. "She gave me three books and told me to read them. If I finish the puzzle and read the books, do you think she'll let me out?"

"Put your ear up to the bottom of the door," Piggy said.

I readjusted my position, thinking I'd become quite a contortion artist in the short time I'd been here. Whoever thought I'd have to carry on conversations through a little hole in the bottom of a door?

"This is what she does," Piggy whispered. "She's going to ask you the title of each book and who wrote it. She'll ask the number of pages in each book. Then she'll ask you what you learned from each book. So memorize the author, title, how many pages, and have something to tell her about what you learned. Got it?"

"I think so. Sounds a little like a book report. Right?"

"Yes, I guess so. But let me warn you, if you don't get those three books right, she'll bring you three more. I understand she's got more than sixty books like that. I mean, it will drive you up the wall, you know!"

"Thanks, Piggy, you're a real friend. And do you think that if—"

"Piggy! Get up off that floor!" a voice yelled from down the hall. "How many times have I warned you not to talk to those girls?"

Piggy took off running.

I peered through the slot in the door and saw Miss Kirk. She hesitated at my door, then turned and walked off.

I went back to the puzzle after finishing every bite of my supper. It was the best meal I'd had. I didn't know if

I was just hungry, or if I was getting used to this food, or what. I knew I was beginning to figure out the system!

This time I didn't stay up all night working though. I never would have been able to keep myself awake. And working on the puzzle did help to occupy my time. Some of the pieces were badly messed up, but I was able to find every one of them, and they all fit. That was one part of the project.

I spent time reading the three books, memorizing the things Piggy had told me Miss Kirk would ask. I guess the whole thing took me two or three days. I lost track of time.

Miss Kirk checked on my progress several times. And the morning after I had finished the puzzle and all three books, she asked if I thought I were ready to get out. I told her I was ready to get out from the first.

"Now," she said, "first of all let's find out what you've learned from your reading." Then she asked me the title of each book, the author's name, the number of pages, and what I had learned from them. I rattled off the answers like a college student on a scholarship. That evil grin on her face slowly melted because I had all the answers. She cleared her throat a time or two and said, "Well, I guess you're ready to get out of here. I'll have to make some arrangements, then I'll be back in a couple of hours."

As she went out, I saw she had some more books in her hand. She hadn't expected me to know the answers. So maybe in a small way I had gotten the best of that old bag!

As I sat there waiting, I was overjoyed. It had worked. And I owed Piggy a big favor. If she hadn't clued me in on what to expect, I probably would have had to read all sixty books.

True to her word, Miss Kirk returned in two hours. As we walked down the hall, even though I was still in prison, I felt liberated from the deepest, darkest hole in the earth. Oh, it felt good.

She led me to another building, through a lounge, down a hallway, and past a number of rooms. None of these rooms had doors on them, but there were two beds in each room.

She led me into one of these rooms where a girl sat on a bed. "Julia," Miss Kirk said, "this is your new roommate, Terri Geiger. Terri, this is Julia Gallo."

I extended my hand, but Julia just sat there staring at me sullenly. So she didn't want me for a roommate; it sure wasn't my fault. I'd rather not be here, either.

"Now, Julia, you mustn't act that way," Miss Kirk remonstrated. "Terri is a good girl and very smart. Very rarely does a girl only have to read three books to get out of the hospital."

Julia didn't respond. She just got off her bed and walked out into the hall.

"What's the matter with her?" I asked.

"Oh, she's a little off in her head," Miss Kirk said, almost offhandedly. "She killed her father and mother and really doesn't make friends too easily."

I jumped back, my eyes wide with sheer terror. "She killed her father and mother? You're putting me in the same room with a murderer who's off her rocker? She ought to be in an institution!"

Miss Kirk laughed. "What do you think we're running here, the Holiday Inn? This is a prison, little girl. We've got all kinds of weirdos in here—murderers, junkies, prostitutes, even thieves like you. We don't choose the people who come here; we take whomever the courts send us. So you might as well get used to it. This is not exactly your Sunday-go-to-meeting crowd."

"Miss Kirk," I protested, "how in the world am I going to sleep in the same room with this murderer? You saw how she treated me. This girl is still mad at the world. She might decide to take out all her frustrations on me some night while I'm sleeping!"

"I'm afraid that's the breaks of the game, little girl," she answered, unmoved. "If you hadn't robbed that pizza place, you wouldn't be facing this problem, now would you? Maybe this will help you learn a big lesson. After all, that's why the judge sent you here, so you'd learn to behave yourself."

"But, but—" My protestations were in vain. She walked out, leaving me alone. The room was bare except for two beds and two dressers. On top of my dresser was a towel, a washcloth, and a bar of soap. I was hoping I'd soon be permitted to shower.

I went over to pick up the towel when I heard footsteps behind me. I looked back, and there stood Julia. She started toward me menacingly, reaching out her hands as if she were going to choke me. Her eyes flashed wildly. Was I going to die already?

When she growled, I jumped up on my bed and backed against the wall. "Don't try anything, Julia," I shouted, "or I'll kick you in the face!"

She edged a little closer. Then all of a sudden she smiled and said, "Hi, Terri! Relax, kid."

I stared. "What did you say?"

She backed off. "I said, 'relax.' "

How was I going to handle this one? Did she have fits that came over her and then left suddenly? How in the world was I going to relax with a murderer?

She flopped onto her bed and, looking up at me, asked, "I bet you just got out of solitary, didn't you?"

I nodded, still standing on my bed, hugging the wall. "You ever been there?"

"Yeah," Julia responded. "I've been there; you've been there; every girl on this ward has been there. It's part of the process that Miss Kirk uses to calm down new girls."

Julia seemed rational enough now. She sure didn't seem like the same person I had met a few minutes ago. I'd better play along.

I eased myself down to where I was sitting on my bed. "Did you have to put a puzzle together?" I asked.

Julia laughed. "Yes. And when I got through, three pieces were missing."

I laughed. It was funny now, but a few days ago it sure had frustrated me. "Man, I know about that," I said. "Did you have to read those books, too?"

"Yes. Miss Kirk said you read only three. I read twelve of them before I caught on. I guess I'm kind of stupid, but I finally got out of there."

I studied my roommate. She just didn't look like a murderer now. I almost liked her. But still there was something strange about her.

She stood up and stepped toward me. Immediately I began edging back toward the wall.

"Terri," she said, "you don't have to be afraid of me. I won't hurt you."

I'll bet that's what all murderers say. I still backed away, clenching my fists to hit her if she attacked me.

"Don't back away from me," she said softly. "What I've got to tell you, I don't want anyone else to hear, especially not Miss Kirk. She may be standing around out there spying on us."

What was Julia getting at?

"Terri, I despise that Miss Kirk," she whispered. "She has no more heart than a cockroach. But I've got to co-operate with her, just like you do. It's part of the system. She always brings the new girls into my room. She expects me to put on a big unfriendly act; then she tells them I'm a murderer. What you saw me do a few minutes ago was nothing but an act. I didn't do it to scare you or because I don't like you; I did it to please Miss Kirk. Next time you see me around Miss Kirk and the other girls, just watch. I'll put on my act again. I'll growl and snarl and even head toward one of the girls. And they'll all scream and start running from me. By this time all the girls here know it's an act. But Miss Kirk doesn't know that they know."

Could this whole thing be another ploy in Miss Kirk's unlimited bag of tricks? Could I trust Julia?

"Terri," she went on, "you're new at all this. But you've got to understand the system. Either the system gets you or you get the system. Sometimes you have to do crazy things in order to survive. If you let prison life get to you, you'll go absolutely loony."

"But I don't know you well enough to trust you," I said.

"That's to be expected," Julia answered. "But for crying out loud, don't stay awake all night worrying about my trying to kill you. I'm no murderer. I didn't kill my parents. You see, Miss Kirk came to me one day and asked for my cooperation. She said if I helped her, I might get out sooner. And she said that she needed help to break these new girls, to put real fear into them. She wanted to use my room for all the new girls. She'd tell them this lie about my being a murderer and all, and I was to act half-crazy.

"I'm really here on a drug charge," she went on. "My boyfriend and me got busted for sales. Well, when Miss Kirk came to me with this scheme, at first I didn't want to do it. But she has ways of persuading people to do things. After all, that's part of the system. You try to gain the favor of the people in charge. So I decided to go along with it."

Was Julia telling me the truth? Or was this her way of throwing me off guard so she really could kill me? I hadn't been here long, but I knew I couldn't trust anybody.

"Now Terri, you've got to play the game along with

all of us," Julia said. "If Miss Kirk comes by and I growl at you, back away from me and act scared. And something else. Tomorrow she'll come by to ask you if you're sleeping well. Tell her a big lie about how you're so scared of me that you're afraid to go to sleep. Ask to be moved to another room. Now that's all part of the game. She won't move you, but she'll think her little scheme is working—and that makes her happy. I think you'll find I'm a good roommate. I won't give you any hassles."

"Julia," I said, "I don't know whether to believe you or not. I'd sure like to get along with my roommate. But I'm so confused over all that's happened to me in the last few days. I mean, my head is spinning. I can't believe what I've been through or that a judge would send me here for my first offense. Are you sure I can trust you?"

She laughed. "Wait here a minute. I'll get another girl."

In a few minutes she was back and introduced me to Ida Shapiro. "Ida," she said, "tell Terri about the game we play."

"You mean the one where you scare us?" Ida asked.

Julia nodded.

"Terri, I don't blame you for wondering," Ida started. "I went through the same process—solitary confinement, the puzzle, the missing pieces, the books, the questions. Then Miss Kirk brought me to Julia. When Julia growled at me after Miss Kirk said she was a murderer, I slapped Julia's face. I was going to show her not to mess around with me. Well, Julia then scratched my face, and we really got into a fight. I guess if Miss Kirk hadn't stopped us, one of us might have killed the other. That wouldn't have been too much of a problem for me. I was in a gang in New York City."

I stared at her uneasily.

"Well, would you believe Miss Kirk slapped me back

into solitary for that altercation? For another week!"

"No kidding," I said.

"Then she brought me back here again. This time when Julia growled, I just gritted my teeth and kept my cool. I didn't want to go back to solitary. But I also had decided something else. If that Julia tried anything, I was going to kill her!"

"Really?"

"Really. Well, you can imagine my response when, after Miss Kirk left, Julia told me it was nothing but a game. So help me, it took me a week to believe it. But it really is the truth, Terri. Ask any of the girls; they'll tell you the same thing. So stay cool, kid, and you'll beat the system."

We chatted a while longer, and Ida left. The whole thing had to be one of the strangest situations I'd ever encountered.

Julia started filling me in on prison life. She really had adapted easily to life here. I was afraid I wouldn't. There's no feeling quite like the loss of your freedom.

The following day when I was walking down the hall, I passed Julia, and she whispered, "Okay, kid, we have to act it out!" I glanced around and saw Miss Kirk following me. Julia growled at me, and I screamed, "Don't hurt me! Don't hurt me!"

Miss Kirk pushed us apart and asked, "What's going on here?"

Julia snarled again, and I raised my fist. "Miss Kirk, please get me away from this beast," I pleaded. "I didn't sleep a wink last night. If you don't move me, I'm going to go crazy!"

I grabbed the lapels of her coat like she was my last hope. "Please, Miss Kirk, do something. This Julia mumbles all the time; she froths at the mouth. I'm terrified of her!"

Miss Kirk jerked my hands from her coat and brushed

it off as though something filthy had touched it. "Serves you right," she announced, and marched off.

Julia growled at me again, and I screamed. But Miss Kirk didn't even turn around. I just knew she had that sick little smile on her face, pleased that her scheme was working so well. Well, when she was far enough away, I stuck out my tongue at her.

Later when the two of us were in our room, Julia said, "Terri, that was fantastic! You ought to get an Oscar for that performance."

Three days later one of the matrons came by and told me my grandmother would be visiting me that afternoon. She said they had had a call from her, and she was concerned about me. The matron warned me not to say anything derogatory about Hudsonville. I sure wasn't going to say anything good about it!

But what really puzzled me, although I didn't tell the matron, was why my grandmother was coming to see me. She lived in Portland, Oregon. Why would she come all the way across the United States to visit me? I hadn't seen her in at least ten years and had never been close to her. I was sure she would be concerned about my being in prison, but why would she come all the way out here to visit me? Something was fishy about the whole deal.

That afternoon another matron led me outside to the reception area where other girls and their visitors were sitting around tables. It was a picturesque spot, not at all like the prison. In fact, I noticed there was only a short fence around the place. Beyond that was a road and cornfields. I could easily jump that fence and escape!

The matron must have read my thoughts. "Miss Geiger," she said, "we have made some compromises for visitation privileges. The visitors aren't really inside the prison when they visit the girls. Then again, the girls are not really on the outside. We want the visiting area to be as pleasant as possible. So we have this picnic area with just that small fence. But in case you're thinking about trying to escape, just look down there to the corner. See that guard? He's got a gun, and it's loaded. That seems to be enough to remind our girls not to try anything."

"Is there another fence beyond that fence?" I asked.

"No, there— oh, I shouldn't have said that. I'm supposed to tell you there's another high fence a little way down the road. You didn't hear that first thing I said, did you?"

I shook my head vigorously, feeling that somehow I'd been let in on a secret. Maybe I could use that information someday!

"Your grandmother called and said she'd be a little late," the matron went on. "Visiting hours will soon be over. Since she has driven so far, we're giving you a little break. You can sit here and wait rather than our having to take the time to get you when she comes. I sure hope she gets here by four because no visitors are allowed in after that."

This wasn't adding up. Why would Grandma drive clear across the United States to visit me? Besides, I didn't ever remember Grandma driving. And why would she come up without my folks? Something wasn't right.

I picked a table near the fence and looked out at the cornfield. It was nice to see the outside again.

Around me other girls were talking to their parents. Would mine ever come to see me? Did they care about what had happened to me? Or were they too embarrassed by it all?

I noticed a trail of dust down the road and then saw a car coming along that little road through the cornfield. I couldn't believe it. Was it? Well, it sure looked like Dad's car. But who was that woman driving it? Was that Grandma?

The car stopped, and I walked over to the fence. The

road wasn't any more than twenty-five feet from the fence. I tried to figure out who the driver was. It probably was Grandma. What was this? She was beckoning me to come to the car! Didn't she realize I was in prison? I couldn't go over that fence!

I stared. Whoever was driving that car wanted me to jump the fence and escape! But who was that old lady?

I glanced around. The guard was looking the other way. I could make it easily. But should I try it?

8

That old lady beckoning for me to escape—was it some type of plot? I would think that if a car stopped beyond the fence, the guard would be on total alert, especially with my standing right at the fence. One leap and I could easily be over it. But he had his back turned! Nobody was even looking my way!

The old lady kept beckoning. I could make out her features, but it had been so long since I'd seen Grandma that I didn't know for sure what she looked like. Why would she risk everything to come to rescue me?

Well, regardless of whom it was, I'd sure like to get out of this place. It might be worth the risk. I put my hands on the fence and tightened my muscles for the leap. But something held me back.

Nearby I saw one of the girls I knew, talking with an older woman. I went over and said, "Hi, Beatrice. Is this your mom?"

"It sure is," she answered. "Mom, this is Terri Geiger. Terri, this is my mom, Mrs. Fahnstock."

"Hope I'm not butting in," I said, "but I need to ask you something, Beatrice. Would you mind coming over here by the fence with me, Beatrice? I found something over there that might be a knife. I was going to pick it up. But I figured if I did that, one of the guards would come running up and slap me into solitary for possessing a weapon. If you'd just come over and take a look at it,

we could confirm what it is and then maybe call over the
guard. Okay?"

"It's probably just some metal left over from the
fence," Beatrice responded. "But, sure, I'll come over
with you. Be back in a minute, Mom."

"Beatrice, now please don't get into any more trouble," Mrs. Fahnstock said. "If it is a knife, you be sure to
let the guard know."

"Don't worry, Mrs. Fahnstock. If it's a knife, I'll call
the guards."

As we walked toward the fence, Beatrice whispered,
"Where is it?"

"Get down here with me," I said.

She began searching through the grass. "So help me,
if I find it, I'm going to keep it," she said. "I've got a
couple of scores to settle with some brainless idiots!"

"Beatrice, now don't run off until I finish," I said.
"There is no knife. But I think I'm being set up. See that
old lady in that car over there?"

She looked, and then smiled.

"What's so funny?" I demanded.

"You want me to tell you who that is?" she asked.

"Well, it's supposed to be my grandmother whom I
haven't seen for ten years. They told me she was coming
today. She keeps motioning for me to escape, but something seems wrong about the whole deal."

"Terri, nobody thought to tell you when you came out
here for the first time. You're right. It's a setup. They do
it to all the new girls the first time they let them out here.
That's really a prison guard dressed up like an old lady."

I stood up and stared. Whomever it was sure did a
good job with the disguise. It really looked like a grandmother.

Beatrice stood up as I yelled across the fence, "Hey,
Grandma, why don't you drive back to Portland and
mend some stockings?"

The car sped off in a cloud of dust. Beatrice was laughing.

I didn't think it was all that funny. Suppose I had jumped that fence. I would have run right into the arms of a prison guard. Then I'd be back in solitary, and probably have my stay here extended for trying to escape! How could an institution stoop so low as to pull a dirty trick like that?

I must have been muttering because Beatrice said, "Simmer down, Terri. They didn't get you. You outsmarted them. And, frankly, I think this grandmother bit is a good idea."

"It's a low-down trick, if you ask me," I retorted.

"There's another way to look at it," Beatrice said. "When your relatives come to visit, we have this nice picnic area to use. And there's just that little fence—it's almost like being out in your own backyard. The administration tries to provide an atmosphere that helps with the visit. Now if all the girls tried to jump that fence, they'd have to stick us in some dingy room. So the guards set up this scheme to use on girls the first time they come out here. If a girl tries to escape, her visiting privileges are taken away. Those who are going to stay and behave themselves have the privilege of coming out here. It's like a reward for behaving.

"Let me tell you something else," she went on. "Visitors can come here seven days a week. Believe me, they've got a great program. It's to our advantage."

Well, she did have a point. But I wasn't all that convinced that they needed to pull a trick like that.

"How many girls have fallen for the trick?" I asked.

"About one a month. Poor girls. All they do is run right into grandmother's arms, and grandmother delivers them to solitary confinement for a month or so."

"You mean every time we're out here visiting, grandmother is out there?"

"No, only when there's a new girl being exposed to the system. You didn't have any visitor; they were just testing you today to see if you'd pass the test. Maybe now they'll let you have visitors, too."

Beatrice went back to her mother, and I sat there a little longer looking beyond the fence to freedom. Oh, if there were only some way I could get out there and be free.

The idea of freedom kept going through my mind the next few days as I planned elaborate escape plots. But nothing was realistic; it was all just a dream.

I was settling into the routine of prison life. I learned they made all our clothes here—out of that sick pea green material. Some of the girls worked in a sewing room and made them. The matrons seemed to delight in issuing us clothes that didn't fit. The fat girls got things that were too tight. We smaller girls got stuff that swallowed us.

The shoes were all the same color—black—and the same style—ugly.

And they were big on schedules. Everybody had to get up by seven. You had to be dressed and showered by half-past, and in the dining room for breakfast by eight. Everything had to be on time.

Those who were late, were put into solitary confinement. It didn't take long to get the message: Be on time!

After I'd been on a ward for a while, they decided I was making enough progress that I could be in a "cottage."

They had several cottages on the grounds. It sounded nice, but they were really individual blocks of cells, each with a housemother over it. She might as well have been called a matron or a guard; it didn't make any difference to us because she sure wasn't a mother. But I guess it sounded better to the people outside to think that we girls were living in cottages with housemothers watching over us!

Inside the rooms in the cottages, it was just like the rest of the prison. The doors had no handles inside. Once they closed a door behind you, you stayed inside until they let you out. It made me feel like a dog or cat—except that maybe dogs and cats got more love and affection.

The cottage I was in had kitchen detail. That meant we either had to cook or clean up after meals. They started me in on cleaning up.

The girls on the kitchen detail were supposed to be tough. I don't know why they put me on it; I wasn't tough. But the last few days before I got this assignment, Miss Kirk seemed to think I was behaving myself. She probably decided she had broken my spirit, and that working with these toughs would continue to put the fear in me.

Mealtime was always under great restrictions. You weren't allowed to talk or whistle or sing. You couldn't even cross your legs under the table. If you did, the matrons would come by and slap you.

The girls on kitchen detail were supposed to sit at the same table together. I'll never forget my first breakfast with them.

We had pancakes. Any resemblance between prison pancakes and the light, fluffy things you've eaten would be purely accidental. I stared down at my three pancakes: tough, flat, totally uninviting.

The girl next to me whispered, "Terri, want one of my pancakes?"

I looked at her plate. Her three were just like mine—only they were burnt, too! I shook my head and turned toward the girl on the other side. I was about to say something when I saw a matron looking our way, so I turned my eyes to my plate.

Now there were only two pancakes on my plate! I looked back at the first girl and discovered she had four on her plate now. I knew she really didn't want my pancake. I'd gladly have given it to her if I thought I could have gotten by with it. But I knew what was happening. She was testing me.

I couldn't let these girls get the best of me, or I'd be in trouble right from the beginning.

The knives they gave us in the dining room weren't sharp ones, but I grabbed my knife, slid it under the table, and pushed it against the girl's leg. "I don't know who you are or what your game is," I said as gruffly as I could and still keep my voice low, "but if you don't put that pancake back, this knife is going right for your throat."

My heart was beating like crazy. What if she called my bluff?

All eyes at that table were riveted on our little drama. She didn't budge.

I applied pressure on the knife, and I felt her leg stiffen. Out of the corner of my eye I could see her hand go under the table. Did she have a sharp knife? After all, she worked in the kitchen and had access to some knives. Besides, some of these girls, especially those from New York City, were real professionals in handling knives and switchblades.

I'd drawn the line. If she started slashing, I'd have to slash too—although I wasn't sure my knife would hurt her.

I applied more pressure under the table and growled, "Baby, I hope you've got a strong neck. When I get through with you, your head is going to roll across the floor! Now you've got five seconds to get that pancake back on my plate. One, two. . . ."

She glanced around to see if any matrons were watching and meekly tossed the pancake back, muttering, "Who wants your nasty old pancake anyway?"

I released the pressure, but I growled, "Don't ever try

that again. Next time I won't give you a chance to put it back!"

I picked up my fork and started eating those horrible pancakes, made somewhat tastier by the sweetness of victory. I had won this battle. But I knew I'd be tested again. And the silence around that table was deafening that morning!

After breakfast my stomach started churning like crazy. I headed for the bathroom and immediately vomited up those pancakes. I don't think it was solely the fault of the food. I think it was more my nervous stomach from that encounter at the table. I couldn't believe what I had been through with the kitchen detail. It wasn't my nature to be a fighter. If we did get into a knife fight, I knew I'd be the loser. I'd had no experience in that. I'd either be killed or be scarred for life. But I also knew that if those girls thought for a minute I was afraid of them, they'd make life totally miserable for me. And nobody here was going to protect me. The matrons and guards really didn't seem to care what happened— as long as we didn't rock the boat for them.

I had to wash dishes and mop floors. My fingers got terribly wrinkled from being in the water so long. I asked for a milder detergent, but they said it was out of the question. They had to have something strong to kill all the germs.

Then I started getting a rash on my hands. I asked for rubber gloves. They laughed at me and called me a softie. The staff just seemed to delight in making things as uncomfortable as possible for us. Maybe that was the reason for prison—to make it so uncomfortable for you that you'd never come back again. But it didn't seem to be working. A lot of the girls at Hudsonville were repeaters who had been there at least once before.

The more I confronted the system, the angrier I got over it. Prison was certainly not helping me in the least.

As the weeks turned into months, everybody seemed to be talking about going before the parole board. But I didn't know when—or if—I'd be going. They seemed to delight in keeping us in the dark about things—even about regulations. You didn't learn about the regulations until after you had broken them.

There was this time when I had received a letter from Sylvia. It wasn't much of a letter—just about her new boyfriend and the kids at school. I felt so envious of her. She was outside, and free!

I wrote her a note and stuck it in my drawer. I didn't have money for a stamp, but as soon as I did, I could mail it. It was the only letter I had received at Hudson-ville. I wondered why my parents didn't ever write.

One day when I got through with kitchen detail, I was told Miss Kirk wanted to see me immediately.

As I walked across the grounds to the administration building, I kept racking my brain, wondering what I could possibly have done wrong now. I was really trying to be good.

It couldn't be that incident over the pancakes, could it? That was a while ago. Besides, I was sure that the girl wouldn't be a stool pigeon. Or would she? Maybe she had told a lie and said I had tried to kill her!

When I got to Miss Kirk's office, she was standing behind her desk. "Sit down," she ordered.

I had learned that when Miss Kirk said, "Sit!" I sat!

She stared down at me, and I stared back. I would never like this woman, and I knew she hated me.

"Don't you know you're on mail restriction?" she started in.

"Mail restriction? I didn't know anything about mail restriction. Has someone been sending me mail, and it's been held up?"

"All the girls who have kitchen detail go on two months' mail restriction," she said. "They are not to receive mail; they are not to send mail. Now you knew that, didn't you?"

"So help me, Miss Kirk, I never heard that before. I wondered why I didn't get any mail, but no one ever told me I was on mail restriction. Honest."

"Well, that's the regulations. You are not to receive or send mail."

"What are you getting at, Miss Kirk?" I asked. "I haven't been receiving mail or sending mail. Even though I didn't know about the restriction, I haven't violated it."

She reached in her desk and pulled out an envelope. Handing it to me, she asked, "What's this, then?"

It was the letter I had written to Sylvia and didn't have a stamp to mail. I'd completely forgotten it!

"Did you write this letter?" Miss Kirk demanded.

Without really thinking, I replied, "No, that's not my letter; I don't know who that person is."

"Miss Geiger, I ought to slap you silly. This is your letter. It is in your handwriting. Furthermore, it has been opened, and your name is signed at the end. We found it in your drawer. What do you have to say to that?"

Now I'd done it.

"Miss Kirk, can I level with you?" I asked. I waited, then I went on. "I want to be an honorable prisoner here. You know I haven't given you any trouble lately. I want to get out of this place. But I did not write that letter. Somebody else must have written it and planted it in my drawer."

"You're lying, Miss Geiger."

I had to lay it on thicker. So I started to sob as I said, "One of those girls on the kitchen crew is out to get me. In the middle of the night I've been awakened by someone in my room with their hands around my throat. And now they've planted that envelope in my drawer to get

me. Miss Kirk, do you have any idea who is trying to kill
me?"

I had to get her mind off that letter. She sat there staring at me.

I repeated the question.

She still wasn't moved. So I dropped to my knees and
grabbed her around the legs, sobbing and pleading,
"Please, Miss Kirk, please! Someone is trying to kill me!
Either that or I'm going out of my mind!"

She grabbed my hair and, yanking on it, screamed,
"Get up, Miss Geiger! Get up before I kill you! I'll not
have anyone sniveling at my feet like this. Now get up!"

The tears streaming down my face now weren't fake
ones. The pain from being yanked up by your hair is
very real! But Miss Kirk was totally unmoved.

"Miss Geiger, you're as phony as everybody else
around here. I don't buy your story. Nobody's trying to
kill you. You wrote this letter. You broke regulations.
Now you're going to have to be punished. Will you
never learn?"

"Punished?" I asked. "I thought I was being punished
by being on the kitchen detail."

"Oh, you don't like being on the kitchen detail?" she
asked sarcastically. "Well, let's see what we can do
about that. Come with me." She grabbed my arm and
started dragging me along after her. When I resisted, she
dug her fingernails into my arm and yelled, "Miss
McKenzie, help me with this one."

A huge woman appeared—big and fat and ugly. She
grabbed my other arm and together they led me down
to—you guessed it—solitary confinement again.

Miss Kirk opened a door, and they pushed me inside.
The door slammed shut.

I let out a bloodcurdling scream, yelling, "I'll kill myself! I'll kill myself!"

I expected the door to fly open and those two women

to start beating me. But I didn't care. I had reached the point of no return. They were not going to humiliate me anymore. How could they get by with making up regulations and not even telling me about them until after I had broken them!

Sure enough, the door opened. I braced myself for the onslaught I knew was coming. But Miss Kirk reached inside, grabbed me by the arm, and pulled me back out into the hall. It worked! They didn't want to explain to the papers about a suicide!

"Did you or did you not write that letter?" Miss Kirk demanded.

Should I keep on lying? No, lying had gotten me back here into solitary. Maybe if I told the truth. . . .

"Yes, Miss Kirk, I did write it. But I didn't mail it. And I didn't know it was against regulations. Nobody ever—"

Before I had finished the sentence, her hand hit flat against my face. Oh, it stung. "Just as I thought!" she yelled. "You're a dirty, filthy liar! I'll bet you haven't uttered one truthful word since the day you were born. We're simply not getting anywhere with your rehabilitation."

With that she started pushing me back into the cell.

"No! No!" I begged. "Don't put me back in there. Please! Please! I'll do whatever you say! Please!"

My pleadings fell on deaf ears, for the two of them gave me a hard shove, and I went sailing into the cell, hitting the wall on the far side. I fell onto the floor in a heap.

Miss Kirk stood in the doorway, looking nine feet tall. "You'll learn!" she screamed. "You'll learn!"

She slammed the door with all her strength, and the noise sounded like the walls would fall in on me. "I'll kill myself! I'll kill myself!" I screamed. But the sounds only echoed through the small cell.

I had such a hatred toward Miss Kirk that I decided I would stay alive so I could kill her first. Then I'd kill myself.

They kept me in solitary for five days. The only way I could keep track was by the meal trays.

Then one day Miss McKenzie came to release me. But instead of heading to my cottage, she seemed to be taking me somewhere else.

"Where you taking me?" I asked.

"To the infirmary."

"But I'm not sick."

"I know. But it's regulations. We have to take you there after you've been in solitary. It has to be on your record."

I laughed. "Solitary makes you sick?"

"Don't knock it, kid. It has a purpose—to teach you a lesson. You don't want to go back, do you?"

I sure didn't. So I decided I'd better cool it. If I had to have an examination on my record after solitary, so be it.

Then it hit me why they had kept me down there for five days. My face had swollen from where Miss Kirk hit me. So by waiting five days until the examination, the swelling would be gone. If they had broken my leg, would I have had to stay in solitary for six weeks?

The nurse was another huge, ugly woman. I don't know where they recruited their help, but they all seemed to be the biggest, ugliest women on earth.

She led me into a room and said, "Take off your clothes."

This was always so embarrassing. It was one thing about prison life to which I never did adjust.

As I unbuttoned my blouse, I heard a girl screaming, "I swallowed a straight pin! I swallowed a straight pin!"

Standing there in the doorway was a terrified little girl. She didn't look much older than twelve. But she had on that sick green uniform. She must have been a prisoner there, too.

The nurse grabbed her and started shaking and slapping her, shouting, "You little idiot!"

The little girl's eyes were big as saucers. She looked scared to death, and that nurse treated her like that! Oh, how I wanted to tackle that stupid nurse. That was no way to treat somebody who had swallowed a pin. Didn't she have any nurse's training?

The nurse grabbed the little girl and marched her to another room, leaving me there by myself. Hey, this was my chance! Could I find a sharp instrument in here? I could hide it on me and use it to kill Miss Kirk the first chance I got. Then I could kill myself and be out of this misery.

I pulled out a drawer and immediately spotted a pair of scissors. That's exactly what I needed!

9

"What do you think you're doing in that drawer?" the nurse thundered from behind me.

Oh, oh! I hadn't expected her back this quickly.

"I'm looking for a magnet," I lied. "That's what you should use to pull the straight pin out of that little girl."

The nurse lunged at me, but I stepped aside. However, she grabbed my blouse at the neck and slapped me hard across the face.

"Don't you know it's against regulations to open any drawer that doesn't belong to you?" she screamed. "The only drawer you are allowed to open is your dresser drawer. No other drawer. Do you understand that?"

"Why are you so uptight?" I argued. "All I was doing was trying to save that little girl's life. What's the matter? You afraid that I was going to show you up because I knew what to do for her and you didn't? Sister, if that little girl dies, they're going to get you and get you good. You're stupid!"

She grabbed the scissors I had my eyes on and held them to my throat. "You little twerp, I ought to take these and poke them right through your throat. Or maybe I just ought to cut your tonsils out—call it emergency surgery—and let you bleed to death! Don't you ever call me stupid again. Nobody calls me stupid and gets by with it!"

Thinking about it, it was pretty stupid of me to call her stupid. She could have finished me off in one fell swoop! Faking a faint, I let my knees buckle, and I crumpled to the floor.

I lay there wondering what she would do next. Her footsteps moved away. Had she gone to check on the little girl?

I jumped up and bolted for the door. But when I got there, a big arm grabbed me right around the neck.

"Terri Geiger, you're the one who's really stupid," the nurse exploded. "I don't know how many girls have pulled that fainting trick. I thought you were smarter than that."

"Where am I? Where am I?" I asked, trying to appear disoriented.

Wham! I felt my head bash up against the wall. She had me by the throat screaming, "I really ought to make mincemeat out of that pretty little face of yours. You little women think you're God's gift to the whole world. Well, you don't impress me none."

The way that nurse was looking at me, I knew she wouldn't hesitate to kill me. I decided I'd better keep my mouth shut. I closed my eyes, hoping that would shut her off. But it just made her madder. "And something else, Miss Geiger," she shouted. "If you breathe a word about what happened here, I'll kill you! I can give you a little injection, and nobody will ever know what happened to you. Now you didn't see any little girl in here yelling about a straight pin! I didn't lay a hand on you! Do you understand?"

I nodded vigorously. "You'd better believe I didn't see one thing," I said. "I was just walking down this hallway. I didn't see anything; I didn't hear anything. Not one thing."

She slowly relaxed her grip. I took a deep breath.

"Come with me!" she ordered.

I obeyed. I didn't want to do anything to get her all upset again. I wondered if she had killed other girls.

She led me to a familiar door—Miss Kirk's. Inside she accused me of attempting to steal drugs while she had to look in on an emergency.

Miss Kirk hit the ceiling. I knew it wouldn't do any good to tell her what really happened. I had no rights. No way would she believe me over the nurse.

Miss Kirk decreed that I would spend two more weeks in solitary. Could I take it that long?

She and the nurse led me back. As we crossed the open area, I looked out toward the big fence. Freedom was on the other side. But would I ever live to see it again?

Those two weeks in solitary had to be the longest two weeks in my life. And solitary wasn't doing me one bit of good. It was making me angrier and angrier at the total unfairness of the system.

I wanted to get out. But how? How could I be sure someone would ever open the door? Miss Kirk didn't come by every day like she did the first time I was in there. The only person I talked to was Piggy when she brought my meals. But they had been getting after her about talking, so she couldn't talk very often.

Somehow I had to get that door open. And it had to be opened from the outside.

Fainting wouldn't work. Maybe if I vomited someone would come in to check on me. I could kill that person and get out.

When my evening meal tray came, I ate everything as fast as I could. Then I got down on my hands and knees by the little opening in the bottom of the door, poked my finger down my throat and tried to vomit. It had to work.

Finally, my stomach started retching. I pushed my

finger down again. Then it all came up. I vomited all over the floor by the entrance to my cell. Now I had to wait.

When I heard footsteps in the hall, it was time for phase two. It was going to be gross, but I had to go through with it. I laid my cheek in all that vomit, right next to the door, and called, "Help me! Somebody help me! I'm dying! I'm dying! I think I've been poisoned!"

The person stopped and looked in, so I rolled my eyes to the back of my head. The stench of the vomit was more than I could take, and I felt my stomach retch again. That should make it all the more convincing.

"Please help me!" I begged. "I've been poisoned!"

Whoever it was jumped up and ran away. Here's hoping they'd come back. I needed to be ready for phase three. I grabbed the sheet off my bed. Whoever opened that door, I'd throw the sheet around her neck and strangle her. And I'd get out!

Sure enough, I soon heard footsteps, so I started moaning as if in pain. But I crouched behind the door, ready to spring at whoever opened that door.

I heard the key in the lock, and the door started to open. Every muscle in my body tensed.

But instead of my jumping at whoever opened that door, a body came hurtling at me so fast that I found myself slammed up against the wall. The door clanged shut, and I was still on the inside.

"Piggy!" I yelled when I saw who it was. "What are you doing here?"

"Terri, you really blew it this time, didn't you?"

"What do you mean?"

"Listen, girls in solitary try everything under the sun to get out. One of their tricks is acting sick. And this is what they always do for that."

"You mean they lock you up with them in solitary?"

"Oh, no. What they do is open the door and push me

in. I'm supposed to play doctor and see if you're sick or not. Now sometimes the girls are really sick, but it's up to me to decide."

"But I'm sick," I yelled. "I think that supper poisoned me. You saw that vomit all over the floor."

"And why were you standing behind the door with that sheet in your hands like you were going to strangle someone?"

When I didn't answer, Piggy said, "You were planning to strangle whoever came in, weren't you? You thought that was the way out of solitary, didn't you? Girl, how stupid can you get? Sit down here. Let me explain a few things to you."

I sat beside her as she continued: "Now this is what I'm going to do. I'll tell them you were sick with an upset stomach but that you're okay now. I'm lying for you, Terri, so don't you blow this one."

Would she really do it? Or was she just trying to calm me down?

"Whatever you do," she warned, "don't start screaming about how you want out of here. If you do, they'll only make you stay longer. And another thing: don't eat your breakfast or lunch tomorrow. Tell them your stomach is still upset. I need coverage on this one."

Could I stand to go without two meals? I guess I'd better. I'd gotten myself into this mess, and Piggy was taking a big chance in helping me. Going without meals at Hudsonville wasn't that big a deal anyway.

Piggy got up, banged on the door, and yelled, "Okay, Miss Watson. I've got this girl settled down."

In a few minutes the door was unlocked, and there stood a matron—a big one—I'd never seen before.

"Miss Watson, I don't think it's food poisoning—just an upset stomach," Piggy said. "I think Miss Geiger will be okay by tomorrow. As you can see, she vomited all over the floor, but I think she's feeling better now."

I stood there staring out that open door. My muscles tensed. Should I leap out to freedom? And if I did, what would they do to me? Keep me in solitary even longer?

Miss Watson didn't respond. She just nodded to Piggy and slammed the door. I waited for someone to come and clean up the vomit which was still all over the floor. After a few hours it became clear that they weren't about to do that. I had made the mess; I'd have to clean it up.

The following day, as I had promised Piggy, I didn't eat breakfast or lunch. My stomach was really growling by suppertime!

Three days later I was taken to Miss Kirk's office again. "Miss Geiger," she said, "I must tell you something about how long you are going to stay here."

Was I going to be released soon? Were they finally getting tired of me?

"Because of your incorrigible behavior since you have been with us," she said, "I am going to have to recommend to the board that you spend at least three more years here. I don't think it would be safe to turn you loose on society."

When she said *three more years,* I came up out of my chair. As I did, she stood, too. And I noticed her fists were clenched. She was ready to hit me if I tried anything.

I slumped back into my chair. "Three years? Three years? The judge sentenced me to only a year. You can't do that!"

"Oh, yes we can, Miss Geiger. The judge sentenced you to a year up here so that you would be rehabilitated. But you haven't been rehabilitated. You are in no condition to go out and face society. You haven't learned the lesson of why society sent you here. You'll just have to stay until you learn to control yourself and follow regulations. All these things you have been doing are all part of your record. The board will have no problem at all keeping you here."

"Miss Kirk, I simply could not take three more years of this place. I'll go stark-raving mad!"

"I don't think you have much choice, Miss Geiger," she said. "And now that we've got that bad news out of the way, I have some good news for you. We're going to let your father visit you today. He's been asking for this privilege for quite some time now, but we didn't feel you were quite ready for it."

"My father is coming to see me? Why?"

"I guess he loves you," Miss Kirk replied, "although I can't for the life of me see why."

Dear old Dad. I had wondered why he hadn't come before. Now I knew—they wouldn't let him come!

That afternoon at two I met Dad in the visitors' area. I enjoyed being outside after all that time in solitary. And it was good to see Dad—even though I could tell he had been drinking again. Or should I say, yet!

He told me about a big change in Mom. He said she'd gotten religion. He didn't know much about it, but she sure was easier to live with than she used to be. She'd been sticking to a diet and had lost twenty-five pounds. On Mom that wouldn't even be noticed but at least it was a start.

"Dad," I said, "have they told you they're thinking about extending my sentence to three more years?"

He looked down at the table, and I could tell he already knew. "Yeah, I had to go through a couple of hours of grilling before they let me see you," he said.

"What do you mean by that?"

"Oh, some woman, I think her name was Kirk, took me into her office and showed me all kinds of charts about your antisocial behavior. She said you were bordering on insanity and that it would be imperative to keep you here to be rehabilitated. Then she brought in a psychiatrist and some other people. Sounds like you've been a real monster since you've been up here. It's a side of you I've never seen before, Terri, and it scares me."

I was furious. "Dad, they've really snowed you, haven't they? Well, all you've heard is their side. I know I did wrong in robbing that pizza place. I did it because we didn't have any grocery money. You remember that?"

He hung his head.

"Well, it was wrong, and I deserved to be punished. I admit that. But this is no place of rehabilitation. The monsters here are that Miss Kirk and her cohorts. Some of the things that have been done to me, you just wouldn't believe. For the least little infraction of the rules, they slap you into solitary confinement. If you don't break the rules, they make up rules and tell you about them later."

I related to him the story of Sylvia's letter. I could tell he wanted to believe me, but he had been raised to respect authority. It didn't occur to him that the prison officials might be the ones who were stretching the truth.

"Dad, this place is hell on earth," I said through my tears. "I have been abused; I have been threatened; I have been humiliated. Dad, I can't take another three years of this place. If something doesn't happen, I'm going to kill somebody, and then I'm going to kill myself!"

Dad stared at me through his red, blurry eyes. "Now, Terri, that's not the way I taught you to handle problems," he said. "You've got to be strong. I didn't realize it before, but I guess because of my drinking and your mother's problems, you've developed some personality characteristics that are harmful."

"Don't try to play amateur psychiatrist!" I exploded. "Our homelife wasn't perfect, but I hadn't turned out all that bad. All those charts and records—it's all part of their setup to control people's lives. Dad, listen to me. If I'm not out of here in a month or so, I'm either going to kill somebody or I'm going to kill myself. There's absolutely no way that I'll spend three more years in this hellhole!"

"Now, Terri, it isn't all that bad. Look. Here you are visiting with me in this nice country air. You don't look like you've lost weight or anything. And I don't see any bruises on you from where these people have supposedly been beating on you. It can't be as bad as you're making it out to be."

People just didn't understand what it was like to be in prison. The hardest part to get over is the loss of your freedom. Knowing you're confined to a cell is one of the worst experiences in the world. I bet if my dad had to spend a week in prison, he'd change his tune. Not so bad? It's awful!

As I turned and looked at the fence and the road beyond, I remembered the trick with the guard disguised as a grandmother. I didn't see any car out there now; I guess all of us with visitors had been through that routine. But suddenly I had a brilliant idea!

I leaned forward and whispered, "Dad, you don't want to see me commit murder and get sent away for life, do you?"

"No, of course not, Terri. All I have ever hoped was that you'd turn out to be a nice girl who'd make your parents proud. Now you did a few little things wrong. But Terri, I believe in you. You can make it. These next three years can be a real turnaround for you. You can get the professional help that I can't afford to get for you. And it's all free here! Take advantage of it so in three years you'll be ready to face society."

That infuriated me, and I grabbed his coat. Jerking him toward me, I said, "You don't understand. If I murder someone up here, they won't have any trouble at all

proving it was premeditated—because that's exactly
what it will be. And they'll send me to the chair, Dad.
I've got to get that superintendent. I've already got a big
switchblade for the job. One of the girl's boyfriends
brought it in for me. The next time I see that Miss Kirk
alone, I'm going to plunge that blade right through her
heart. And a lot of people up here are going to be ap-
plauding me for doing it. Do you understand what I'm
saying, Dad?"

His eyes grew wide. "Terri, Terri! Don't do that!
Don't kill! You won't stand a chance!"

"Dad, that's what I'm trying to tell you. This place is
turning me into a vicious murderer. Take a look at your
little girl. I wasn't like this when they sent me up here.
This is what Hudsonville Training School has done to
me!"

"Maybe you and I should go and talk to Miss Kirk together," Dad said lamely. "She'll help you. She seems so
understanding."

"Understanding?" I screamed. "That woman has
slapped me and hit me and humiliated me in more ways
than I can name. If you take me to her office, I'll kill her
right in front of you!"

"Terri, stop acting this way! What am I going to do
with you?"

"Dad, there's only one way out of this mess," I said.
"You've got to help me escape."

He blinked and drew back in surprise.

"How in the world are you planning to do that?" he
asked.

"I know this place seems to be carefully guarded," I
said "but there is one weakness. It's because of a plan
they've devised to trap new girls." I told him about the
grandmother plan.

"What about the guard over there—the one with that
rifle?" he asked.

"He doesn't do a thing when the grandmother plan works," I explained. "In fact, he turns his back. After all, the girl is running right into the arms of another guard, only that guard is disguised as a grandmother."

"That's dirty," he said.

"Yes, and the girl gets solitary for a month," I added, realizing that maybe I was finally getting him to come my way.

"All you're going to have to do, Dad, is drive up in your car and stop on the other side of that fence. Just dress up like a grandma. I'll be by the fence. Just motion for me to come. The guard will think you're a guard and won't do a thing. I'll leap over the fence, and we'll take off. You will have rescued your little girl from a fate worse than death!"

"You really think it'll work, Terri?"

"Dad, I know it'll work. Just beyond that fence is freedom for me."

He sat there silently for the longest time, thinking. Then he said, "Terri, it's a terribly long shot. I don't think it'll work. I mean, that guard isn't going to fall for it; he'll know whether it's planned for that week or not. And my car won't be like the one they—"

"Your car is exactly like the one they use," I interrupted. "That's one of the beauties of this plan. In fact, that's how they almost got me. I really thought it was your car out there!"

His eyes brightened. Then they fell. "Terri, if this goes wrong, I'll go to jail, too. I may get thirty years. It's an awfully big gamble for such a little thing. If we blow it, we're both in big trouble."

He was weakening. I had to apply more pressure.

"Dad," I said, taking his face in my hands and making him look right into my eyes. "If you don't go through with this, I want you to take a good look at me. This will be the last time you see your little girl alive.

When you walk away from here, I'm going to kill that dreadful Miss Kirk. And then I'm going to kill myself to save the state the expense of a trial. I know one thing for sure: I'm not going to take this place any longer!"

"You can't be serious," Dad protested.

"Dad, I won't lie to you. It's either this escape plan, or I'm going to end it all. There's no hope for me here. So take one last look!"

Dad stared at me. Then I got up and slowly started to walk away. Would he call me back?

"Terri, come here," he called.

"I'm really afraid you mean it," he went on. "I'll try it. But if it doesn't work, I don't know what I'm going to do!" He was almost in tears.

"Dad," I encouraged, "it'll work. I know it. It's got to. But be sure you call the prison and tell them you're coming to visit me. Otherwise I can't get into this area. It's restricted."

"I understand," he said. "I'll be out there on that road at exactly two next Friday afternoon. I'll have on a wig and a dress. When I see you standing by the fence, I'll beckon you to come. And, Terri. . . ." He paused. "I don't know much about praying, but if you've ever prayed, you'd better do it then. Because if this doesn't work, it'll be curtains for both of us."

What would happen if we blew it? I knew what I would do. I'd kill myself.

I thanked Dad for his help and reassured him that it would all work out. I wished I could be as sure as I sounded. So many things could go wrong. For one thing, what if there were a new girl meeting visitors that Friday? It would sure arouse suspicions to have two grandmothers out there! Well, there was nothing I could do about that—except hope and pray.

The next week was so long. I was careful to obey

every rule. I sure didn't want to risk getting thrown in solitary this week!

When Friday finally came, I was told that my dad was coming to visit me again. I acted surprised, telling the matron that I hadn't expected him back for at least a month. She told me he had sounded anxious to share something with me.

"Maybe he's bringing bad news?" I asked.

She tried to reassure me that everything was okay. I thought, *If this scheme works, everything will really be okay!*

Just before two the matron led me out to the picnic grounds. I picked a table close to the fence and waited.

The clock on the administration building struck two. I looked down the lonely dirt road and spotted a cloud of dust getting bigger and bigger. It looked like Dad's car. But was it the guard disguised as a grandma? Was there a new girl out here today? I hadn't noticed one, but. . . .

I looked down at the guard. He had spotted the approaching car, too. He seemed to be clutching his gun tighter. Did he know something was up? Had someone overheard our escape plans and reported them to the authorities? Was this going to be the end for Dad and me?

10

As I walked over to the fence, I had to laugh to myself. I could see it really was Dad, but he looked so crazy in that disguise. He had used way too much makeup and didn't have it on properly. But the crowning feature was his bright peroxide-blonde wig. It was almost ridiculous.

I glanced over, and the guard was still staring intently. What could I do to get his attention away from me?

Then I heard someone behind me calling my name. I turned around to see Barbara Weissman, my house-mother.

"Terri, you'd better get away from that fence!" she yelled.

Oh, no! Did she know I was planning to jump the fence and take off with my father? Who could possibly have told her? I hadn't breathed a word to anyone.

"Terri, I know what's going on," she said, coming up to me. "I saw that woman beckoning you to come. I'm going to tell Miss Kirk about this right now!"

Mrs. Weissman hadn't been here very long. Didn't they fill the staff in on that ploy they used to test new girls? Were they afraid word might leak out if they told too many people?

I had to test her and see how much she knew. "Haven't they told you? That so-called old lady out there is really a prison guard," I said. "It's nothing but a setup to trick new girls."

She leaned close and whispered. "Terri, I know all

about that setup. But we're worried because word has gotten around outside of prison about it. That person in that car is not the guard. I don't know who it is."

"No, come on," I protested, "that's the guard. That looks like the same person they used when they tested me."

"Terri, I know what I'm talking about," she went on. "The guard, Mr. Schwald, uses a gray wig, not a blonde wig. And he does a much better job of putting on makeup."

Oh, no! Now would she yell for the guard and give away my escape plan? I had to get her interest elsewhere—right away. So I said, "Let's turn our backs on him and ignore him. He'll probably realize what's going on and leave."

"I don't know why I'm telling you this, Terri," Mrs. Weissman went on, "but we've had some problems with pimps trying to get girls out of here. They disguise themselves as big brothers, fathers, uncles, grandfathers, and you name it. If a pimp succeeds in getting a girl, he puts her on the street as a prostitute. The girl can't run to the authorities because she is an escapee. And you know what escapees get—long prison terms. And that guy out there looks like a pimp, Terri!"

"Really?" I asked in surprise. "You really think he looks like a pimp?"

"He sure does!"

I could hardly keep a straight face. Wait till I told Dad!

"I think I'd better go get Miss Kirk," she said. "She'll want to know about this."

When she said go, an idea struck. It was a good way to get her out of the picture. "You're right, Mrs. Weissman, he does look like a pimp," I said. "I think you'd better go get Miss Kirk, or one of these girls is going to get into deep trouble."

As she headed toward the building, I walked back to the fence. The guard was still eyeing the situation suspiciously, but I knew it had to be now or never. I'd talked Dad into this caper. In a few minutes Miss Kirk would be back, and Dad would be in big trouble.

I took the fence in one leap. Running at top speed, I headed for Dad's car, wondering if at any moment I would hear the report from the guard's rifle and feel the bullet sink into my body.

Dad read the action, threw the back door of the car open, and was ready to take off as soon as I jumped in and slammed the door.

He must have jammed that accelerator clear to the floorboard. We took off in a cloud of dust with gravel spraying everywhere. I expected the guard to start shooting at the car, but he didn't. The idiot thought I was escaping with another guard! We'd made it!

My exhilaration was short-lived, however, because when Dad turned a corner, there was a car completely blocking the little country road.

"It's a blockade!" I screamed. "Run it!"

"I can't!" Dad shouted back. "There are ditches on both sides of the road. We'd overturn and be killed!"

I vaulted into the front seat screaming, "If we stop now, they'll get us both. For life!"

Dad slowed as we approached the car. "Terri, get some sense into you!" he yelled. "The guy standing by that car doesn't look like an officer!"

I looked. Sure enough, he was dressed in jeans and a straw hat. But that didn't mean. . . . We had no choice.

Dad braked to a halt, and I jumped out. "Mister, move that car now!" I ordered.

"Whoa there, young lady," he responded. "Where's the fire?"

I couldn't blurt out that I was escaping. So I yelled,

"My mother's about to have a baby! She's in the back-seat! We've got to hurry!"

That farmer sprang to his car in an instant, wheeled it around, and had it out of our way. He must have known what having babies was all about!

I jumped back into our car, and Dad sped off in an-other cloud of dust. I was cursing the delay. It might have given the prison authorities just enough time. . . .

I had just started to relax when up ahead I spotted a police car parked alongside the road. Dad saw it, too.

"Hang on!" he shouted.

I grabbed the wig and clamped it on my head. Maybe it would fool the cops. I realized later how stupid that was. I still had on my prison uniform.

Dad wasn't taking any chances. The next thing I knew we were bounding across a cornfield. That had to be one of the roughest rides I've ever had, slamming up and down in that seat with my head actually touching the roof of the car. But when we looked back, we didn't see any cops following us. Maybe they weren't aware I had escaped! Oh, I hoped not. Every minute now was pre-cious.

We finally came to another road on the opposite side of the field. Dad turned onto it and slammed the acceler-ator to the floor again. We must have been doing ninety—on a gravel road. "Slow down!" I shouted, "or you'll kill us both!"

He slowed slightly, and I breathed a little easier. Still there was no sign of those cops.

Pulling a big wad of bills out of his pocket, Dad handed it to me. "Here," he said, "take this. If we get stopped, you go one way; I'll go the other. Go to Buffalo and check in at the YWCA. I'll meet you there."

I stuffed the money into my pocket, wondering where it had come from. But I didn't have time to ask. I was listening for sirens when I heard the whine of a train whistle. Up ahead I saw the railroad tracks across the road. Then I spotted the train approaching! We weren't going to make it!

Dad clamped the steering wheel in both hands and stared straight ahead at the crossing. If we had to wait for that freight, we would lose the head start we had on the cops. But I had seen too many movies. I just knew we'd get across ahead of the train and be safe.

The engineer had spotted us and was giving a strong, steady blast on the whistle. He knew we weren't going to make it.

"Dad! Dad! Stop! Stop!"

"Hang on!" he yelled.

To this day I don't know how he did it. He must have slammed on the brakes, because I realized the car was skidding. Then we started to spin. I gritted my teeth and grabbed the edge of the seat to brace myself. I knew we were going to slam into the side of the train.

I felt the car leave the road and bounce through a field to a stop. I couldn't believe it. We hadn't overturned! We hadn't crashed!

I wasn't even scratched. But Dad was slumped over the steering wheel. The train roared on by.

I looked back toward the road. Would the police car catch up with us now? Were my hopes of freedom to last only a few minutes! Now what would become of me? and of Dad?

Dad—I'd better see if I could help him. Maybe he was seriously injured—or dead!

Suddenly he sat back up in the seat and exclaimed, "That was as close as I ever want to come to a train!"

"Are you okay?" I asked.

"Yes, I guess so. Only petrified, that's all. And you?"

"I'm fine. But that was one of the dandiest examples of driving I've ever seen!"

"Don't ask me to do it again," he laughed nervously. "I don't remember what I did."

Saying something about getting out of there, Dad turned the key. The engine roared to life. Wonderful! Maybe the car hadn't been damaged.

He pushed the accelerator. We heard a lot of noise, but we weren't moving. I looked back. Mud was flying everywhere. I opened the door and stepped out to see if I could assess the situation. My feet sank in deep mud. I looked around and realized we had stopped in a low, muddy spot in the field. The mud had probably saved our lives, but now it held us fast.

Dad started to cuss. "Let's get out of here quickly, Terri. We're still too close to that prison. They're out looking for us by now. We'll never get the car free without a tow truck."

He pulled the keys out of the ignition, went around to the trunk, opened it, and pulled out two small, soft-side suitcases. Handing one to me, he said, "Your clothes are in that one."

We sloshed through that mud back to the main road. "Do you know where we are now and where we're headed?" I asked.

"I haven't the foggiest," he responded. "But I think Buffalo is that way. We'll be close to the state line there."

We agreed to walk down the road until we spotted someone coming. I wondered if the authorities had their bloodhounds out looking for me. Prison! What would it be like if they caught me now? I didn't even want to think about it. I knew I'd be in solitary for an eternity!

The mud on our shoes was holding us back, so we took a moment to clean it off in the grass alongside the road. It was while we were there, partially hidden, that we heard the car coming toward us. We jumped back

into the cornfield until Dad ascertained that it wasn't a
police car—just someone driving along the road. So we
hurried to the road, stuck out our thumbs, and waited.

The car slowed to a halt beside us. Dad and I jumped
into the backseat. The woman driving turned around
and smiled. "My, my, what do we have here?" she
asked.

I glanced at Dad. He did look strange with makeup all
over his face. Then I realized I was the one wearing the
wig! We must have been a crazy sight.

"Ma'am, my daughter and I had car trouble up the
road," Dad explained. "I had a blowout, and the car
careened into a mudhole in the field back there. You
didn't happen to see it, did you?"

"Sure did," the woman answered. "You really must
have been traveling. I noticed you really went a distance
into that field. How fast were you going?"

"Oh, about seventy-five," Dad responded.

I wished he hadn't said that! If this woman had any
sense, she knew there was a prison around there, and
she'd suspect I'd escaped. Especially if we were traveling
that fast on a gravel road. I'd better change the subject.

"You see, my mother just had a baby yesterday," I
said. "The hospital just called us and said there were
some complications. Dad got pretty nervous about it
and was driving faster than he should have."

The woman didn't say anything else—just drove
along. But I got this strange feeling—call it intuition if
you want—that something was dreadfully wrong.

"How far are you going?" she asked.

Now I was in a jam. I didn't know how far it was to
the next town or even what the name of the town was.
So I responded, "Oh, just up to the hospital." I figured
there would be only one hospital in this part of the country.

Once again no response from the woman. My heart

kept beating faster and faster.

At a stop sign, the woman turned right. At the next road she made another right. I have a good sense of direction, and I had a sneaking suspicion we were heading right back to the prison.

I leaned forward and growled, "This is not the way to the hospital!"

I saw her tighten her grip on the steering wheel. I knew we were in trouble.

"Where are you taking us?" I demanded.

No answer.

I brought my index finger up to the back of her head and said, as gruffly as I could, "Ma'am, you'd better start saying your prayers. What are you trying to pull on us?"

She started to shake violently. "Okay, I knew you had escaped when I first saw you on the road," she said.

"Escaped?" I responded. "What are you talking about?"

"I've visited that prison," she said. "I've seen the green outfits the girls wear. I recognized the color. You've escaped, haven't you?"

I jabbed my finger into the back of her head and screamed, "Keep your mouth shut and turn this car around now!"

Would she call my bluff? If she kept going, what could I do? I held my breath.

She stiffened, but she didn't slow down or attempt to turn around.

"Say your prayers, lady, it's all over!" I screamed.

She slowed, and I yelled, "Pull over and stop!"

She rather meekly obeyed. I vaulted into the front seat beside her, yelling, "Keep her covered, Dad! If she tries anything, blast her brains all over the windshield!"

Her mouth dropped open, and her eyes bugged out.

"Now, lady, get out of this car and walk straight up

that road. If you turn around, so help me, my dad is going to blast you. You're lucky he hasn't killed you already. He's been in the penitentiary, and he won't hesitate to kill to keep from going back."

Trembling, she opened the door, slid out, and started walking straight ahead. Dad leaped over the seat, slid behind the wheel, made a U-turn, and we took off again. I glanced back toward the woman. She was still walking straight ahead, afraid even to look around. Our plan had worked!

Dad had that car up to eighty in a few minutes. "Slow down!" I told him. "The next thing you know, we'll be arrested for speeding! Then they'll find out I escaped from prison and you helped me and that this is a stolen car. We can't afford to arouse any suspicions!"

That slowed him down.

Before long we were on the interstate. Dad kept the car exactly at fifty-five. I kept watching for cops who might be following us, but so far we had made it okay.

At the first town of any size we came to, we decided it might be where we could hole up temporarily. I'd never been to Syracuse before, but Dad said he knew of a hotel downtown. He thought that would be safer than a motel along the highway.

So we drove into town, parked the car some distance from the hotel; and walked the rest of the way. I slapped the wig back on Dad's head so he wouldn't look quite as ridiculous in his makeup. We grabbed the suitcases and hurried through the streets of downtown Syracuse. On up ahead was the hotel.

Dad had hardly said a word the whole time. He was risking everything for me, and I had to let him know I appreciated it. "Thanks, Dad," I said. "It's a good thing you got me out of there, or I know I would have killed somebody. You saved my life."

He smiled, and that smile spoke volumes.

Inside the hotel Dad told the clerk, "I'd like two rooms."

The clerk stared at us. That was when I first realized that I still had on my uniform: green sweatshirt with *State Training School* stenciled across it, green bermudas, old black shoes. Dad was dressed in that ridiculous disguise.

"What is this? Some kind of joke?" the clerk asked.

I had to come up with a quick answer, or he'd call the police immediately. "You see, mister, I just escaped from the state training school," I explained. "My dad disguised himself as a woman and rescued me."

Dad kicked me in the shins. I knew he was horrified that I was telling the truth. But I figured if I told the truth, the clerk would think it was indeed a big joke.

"You did what?" he asked in surprise.

"My dad just pulled off one of the biggest heists in the history of New York," I said. "He disguised himself as a woman and helped me escape from the state training school, where I was being held against my will." I dropped my voice to a whisper and told him confidentially, "Dad's going to set up a business. He'll make a lot of money springing people from prison."

The clerk heehawed. I laughed, too, and kicked Dad so he'd join in. The truth was too preposterous for the clerk to believe.

When Dad laughed, the clerk said, "Mister, would you take me as your partner? The pay I get for this job is lousy. But I'll bet you make a lot of money springing people from the pen. Sounds like a great idea!"

If that clerk only knew!

Dad paid for the rooms in cash. When he pulled out a wad of money about the size of the one he had given me, I wondered again where he got it. But this sure wasn't the time to ask.

The clerk pushed two keys toward us. I grabbed one, and Dad grabbed the other. We headed for the fourth floor.

When I opened the door and walked across my room, I suddenly realized it and exclaimed, "I'm free! I'm free!" I looked around for Dad, but he wasn't there. Evidently he had gone to his room. Well, we were both pretty worn out from the hectic experience we had been through. He probably wanted to rest. I know I did.

I took a big leap and flopped onto the bed. It felt so good to be on a real bed—so soft, so different from prison.

I had just closed my eyes, savoring the delight of this moment, when the phone rang. Should I answer it? Who knew I was there? Who could possibly be calling? Oh, sure; it was probably Dad, wanting to set a time to go get something to eat.

When I whispered, "Hello," into the receiver, I heard Dad yell, "Terri, we've got to get out of here! Now! Something is wrong!"

"Dad, where are you?"

"I'm in a phone booth across the street. As soon as you walked into your room, I had this feeling that something was wrong, so I came down here. Terri, we're in trouble. We've got to move right now."

"But where will we go? The cops will be everywhere looking for us. You said you thought we'd be safe in downtown Syracuse."

"I know. I know. But that woman has sounded the alarm. The cops have probably already tailed our car and picked it up. That means they'll be here in a few minutes. In fact, I can see one from right here. He's watching the hotel!"

Was Dad being overly suspicious? Would the cops be out in big numbers tracking us down? Was it a coincidence that there was a cop watching the hotel?

I couldn't take a chance. We had to get away.

"Don't bring your suitcase," Dad cautioned. "It will just arouse more suspicions. Come down here across the street where I am. We'll get a cab to the airport and fly somewhere. But be quick, Terri! They're moving in on us! I know it!"

Poor guy! He was really paranoid. But suppose he were right! I sure didn't want to go back to prison.

After Dad hung up, I took a longing look around my room. It was so quiet, so peaceful, so different from the prison. Why couldn't we just stay here a couple of days?

But I knew Dad wouldn't hear of it. I'd gotten him into this mess, so I'd better go along with his hunches— or he'd never forgive me.

I took the elevator down. As I walked across the lobby, the clerk yelled, "Where are you going so soon?"

"My dad is planning another prison escape," I replied slyly. "I've got to go help him."

The clerk laughed. "You two are really something else," he said. "I've had all kinds of people in here, but I've never had a couple like you. What's your game, anyway?"

I didn't answer. I didn't know what my game was. All I knew was that we had to get out of there.

Dad signaled me from across the street. When traffic cleared, I walked over. "Quick! We've got to get away!" he said. "I know they're after us!"

He started running down the street, and I took off after him, running to try to keep up. A block away he spotted a cab, hailed it, and ordered the driver to take us to the airport, pronto.

That cabdriver really knew how to get through traffic, and we were at the airport in what I guess must have been record time. Dad pulled out that wad of money again to pay him.

At the ticket counter Dad told the clerk we wanted the next flight out of town.

It was almost a remake of the clerk at the hotel. This one looked at Dad, then at me.

"The mob is after us," Dad explained. "We just got into this town, and I ran into this guy in a phone booth." He lowered his voice. "Would you believe he had a machine gun?"

The clerk blinked. If I didn't say something, Dad was going to ruin this whole thing.

I had glanced at the board announcing arrivals and departures and noticed that the next flight out was to Chicago. So I said, "Excuse me, sir, but my father has had an emotional breakdown. We actually are going to Chicago. His psychiatrist, Dr. Wilkes, is there. I'm taking Dad there to see him. He seems to be the only one Dad has any confidence in."

"And you should have seen the size of that machine gun!" Dad went on. "I mean, I know the mob is out to kill us. You've got to help us!"

I really wished Dad would shut up. If he didn't, this clerk would call airport security. Then it would be all over for us.

"I'm sorry for being so disruptive," I whispered. "But I've got to humor him to get him on the plane—even to the extent of his wearing that crazy outfit and my wearing this one. Thank you for being so understanding. He's really harmless, I assure you."

The clerk looked at me, then at Dad, and back at me.

"Two tickets to Chicago," I repeated.

He turned and looked down toward the end of the counter. I held my breath. Was he looking for airport security? What were we going to do now?

11

When the ticket clerk started toward the end of the counter, I glanced at Dad. The two of us did look ridiculous. But did clerks get wary of every suspicious-looking person? Was he afraid we might be hijackers? Or had he received word from the police to be on the lookout for us?

At this point there wasn't much to do but wait and see. But I kept an eye peeled for airport security headed our way.

The clerk walked back from the office where he had gone. "Are you sure you want to go to Chicago?" he asked.

Dad answered in a high-pitched voice like a woman's: "Yes, sir. You see, sir, we're on our way home. My daughter ran away, and I had to come here to bring her back home."

Dad's voice was so absolutely ridiculous that I was ready to burst out laughing. I caught myself in time, but not before a faint smile started to break on my face.

Dad screeched again, "It will be so wonderful to have our daughter back home again!"

I studied the clerk for his response. Nothing. Then all of a sudden the whole crazy situation got to me, and I broke out laughing. The clerk tried to avoid my look. I could see him stifle a laugh—then another. Finally he couldn't help himself, either, and he snickered. Dad was still somber as a judge. By now I was laughing so hard I was crying. And the clerk had quit trying to hold back his laughter. He was going on as though this were the funniest thing he had ever seen.

Dad came down with his foot on mine. I got the point and shut up. It wasn't that easy for the clerk, however. "If you ask me," he said between laughs, "you two have probably escaped from some mental institution. But you both look harmless enough."

You can believe that when he started to punch the buttons to make out our tickets, I was plenty relieved. So far, so good.

Dad paid cash for the tickets, and we headed toward the gate. We had an hour until our flight left.

We really needed to get out of the crazy clothes we were wearing. But Dad had told me to leave my suitcase at the hotel. I sure didn't want to knock somebody off just to get clothes. And it would be foolish to try to steal a suitcase. We'd have airport security on us in nothing flat. It was more important to get out of state.

As we headed to the gate, I noticed a small shop that looked as though, among all the souvenirs and everything else, it might have some women's clothes. I told Dad I was going in.

I quickly located a skirt and a T-shirt in my size. So it said *Syracuse* on it. It was better than *State Training School!* I even found a pair of leisure shoes in my size.

When I went to the counter, the clerk looked at me in surprise. "It's my Halloween outfit," I explained.

She didn't say a word. Maybe she was used to all sorts of weirdos. Anyway, I wasn't about to say anything else.

She rang up the merchandise. I paid from the wad of money Dad had given me, and she slipped the things into a bag. As I headed out the door, I wondered if she would call the cops. Maybe I was getting as paranoid as Dad. But I knew I had to be careful. I sure would do anything to keep from ending up back at that training school.

I found the women's room and made a quick change. Fortunately the clothes fit perfectly. I decided to take my old things in the bag with me. After all, if someone located them just after we took off, they could still call ahead to Chicago and have us arrested when we landed.

Dad was waiting for me, anxiously looking at the clock. "It's okay," I told him, "we still have forty-five minutes. And I sure feel a lot better to be out of that green uniform. I don't care if I never see another piece of green clothing!"

But Dad was still in that ridiculous disguise. We had to do something about him.

"You've got a change of clothes in your suitcase?" I asked.

"Yes, but I've been wondering how to handle this," he replied. "If I walk into the men's room, everybody is going to start yelling and shouting. Maybe some nut will even try to rape me. But if I go into the women's room, *I'll* probably start screaming. Either way I'm going to come out looking different from when I went in. But I'm going to have to do something. I've got to go to the bath-room!"

We talked back and forth for a few minutes about which would be the best place, or if we should wait until we were on the plane. We decided that might create more questions from the stewardesses, and it would be impossible to get away from the situation once we were on the plane.

"You'd better go to the men's room," I finally told him. "In the long run that will create less problems. Maybe the men in there will simply think you're a little, you know. . . ."

"They'd better not," Dad replied angrily, "or I'll bust them with my purse!"

"Pull some pants and a shirt out of your suitcase," I told him. "Hold them up in front of you when you go in. If anybody sees you, tell them you were at a costume party."

Dad headed for the men's room, and I waited, hoping there wouldn't be a lot of commotion. We sure didn't want anything to attract attention to us and bring around the security police. Things had been going too well for us to get fouled up now.

A little later when Dad came out, he looked so different. Maybe now we wouldn't have to answer all these stupid questions about the way we looked. Maybe if we had taken time to change sooner, we would have been better off. But then, would the delay have enabled the cops to catch up with us? Well, at least we were changed now.

"Flight four fifty-one is now ready for boarding at gate three," a voice said over the intercom.

We hurried in that direction. In moments we were on the plane waiting for takeoff. I'd feel a lot more secure when we were airborne. And even more secure when we could disappear into Chicago.

As we fastened our seat belts, Dad whispered, "We'd better come up with some fictitious names."

"Yes, let's be more imaginative than the 'John Smith' you came up with when you bought the tickets and registered at the hotel. I meant to tell you that that's too obvious."

"Yes, I knew that," he whispered back, "but I couldn't think of anything else. You've got to admit that this has been a pretty hectic day!"

"Okay, but how about something like Benson?" I suggested. "And I'll be your daughter Sissie. Okay?"

"Great!"

When we finally took off, I settled back to relax. All the nervous tension of the escape was really getting to

me, and it felt so good just to be able to breathe free air!
I wondered about what Chicago would be like. I'd never
been there.

The stewardess came by and asked if we'd like something to drink before dinner. It was a routine question,
but I noticed her looking questioningly at Dad. I
glanced over and realized the reason for her puzzlement.
Dad had forgotten to take off his makeup!

"It's okay, ma'am, he's harmless," I whispered to her.
"He sort of drifts in and out of reality. I had to let him
put on some of my makeup to humor him and get him
on the plane. But he's harmless. He'll be okay. I think
that in a few minutes I can reason with him and get him
to take off the makeup."

Her expression didn't change. So to get rid of her, I
said, "I'll have a Coke, and my dad will have black coffee."

The stewardess moved on. But when I glanced back
down the aisle, I caught her looking in our direction. She
shrugged her shoulders, and I shrugged back. I made a
circular motion next to my head with my finger. She
smiled. I knew then it was okay.

I pulled my state-training-school sweatshirt out of the
bag and had Dad use it to get the excess makeup off his
face. Then he went back to the rest room and washed
up. Now maybe we'd be through with having to act
crazy!

I cleaned up everything of the dinner they served. It
had been quite a while since I had eaten, and the food
tasted heavenly after what I had been getting.

It was late when we arrived in Chicago, since we
weren't on a nonstop flight. In the terminal we spotted a
bank of telephones connecting to various hotels. Dad
called the Palmer House, and they had rooms available.
The airport limousine—it was really a bus—took us
right to the door.

We spent two days at the Palmer House. It was such a nice place. I even got in some shopping and bought a few more clothes, so at least I had something besides that T-shirt that reminded me of Syracuse.

But Dad was really getting nervous about our staying in one place. He suspected that every person he saw was a plainclothes cop. With any little noise, he'd jump sky-high. Then he told me he thought we'd better move on because "they" were closing in on us.

"Terri," he told me, "we've got to have an escape plan. If anybody knocks on the door, you go over and open it quickly. I'll come up on the other side and hit him. Then we'll head for the fire escape. Cops always guard the front door. So if we try to run out the front door, they'll shoot and kill us. So we'll use the fire escape. You got that?"

"Dad, take it easy, will you?" I answered. "You're getting paranoid. Nobody is going to knock on that door. Nobody knows we're in Chicago. We've given them the slip. Now everything is going to be okay. They don't know we're here."

"Oh, yes they do!" he responded. "There's an all-points bulletin out for us. I just know it. They've got our description. They know you've escaped. And they probably suspect me. They'll check at our house in Kent. Maybe Mom has even reported me missing. I didn't tell her what I was going to do."

"Dad, please stop it," I said. "You are really making me nervous. And when that happens, I can't think straight. We've got to keep our wits about us. Now let's relax. Okay?"

I sat back into the overstuffed chair. I needed to get him thinking about something else. Maybe if I talked about Mom. Oh, hey, this would be a good time to ask him where he got the money.

"Dad, I've been meaning to ask you about—"

Bang! Someone knocked hard on our door.

Dad leaped sky-high. And this time I did, too. Was he right? Had the authorities trailed us here?

Someone kept pounding on the door.

"Terri," Dad whispered, "there's no way they're going to take me alive. This is a crazy deal I've gotten involved in, but I sure couldn't make it in jail. You follow our escape plan that I told you about. When we get out, we'll run for our lives!"

I tiptoed to the door as Dad got a chair from the desk and held it over his head, ready to strike. I sure hoped he wouldn't miss. I knew that if you swung a chair at a cop, he'd probably pull the trigger of his gun first and ask questions later.

I grabbed the door handle firmly, unlatched the lock, turned the knob, and jerked open the door. Then I jumped back. I knew they were going to pounce on us.

As the door flew open and I was jumping back, I spotted a lady in a uniform. But not a police uniform. "Maid service," she said. "You need more clean towels?"

I gasped. I wasn't expecting the maid; I was expecting the police!

Without answering I moved back over and slammed the door. Dad looked pretty silly holding that chair up over his head.

"Relax," I said. "It was only the maid."

"Maybe; maybe not," he responded. "I don't think it was the maid. They usually call 'maid service' when they knock. I think that was a police officer disguised as a maid."

Poor Dad. The maid must have been in her sixties. She looked too tired to do any cleaning, much less be a police officer in disguise.

"Put down the chair, Dad. She's no police officer."

"Terri, I'm trying to tell you that that was no maid.

She's a police officer. Now that she knows we're here, she's gone to get help. There'll be a whole bunch of them here in a minute!"

He made me open the door again and check the hallway. "It's clear," I told him. "I don't see anyone, not even the maid."

"Good!" he responded, setting down the chair. "Now let's get out of here!"

I did talk him into taking the elevator to the lobby. We got out and looked around. Apparently there were no cops guarding the door—at least none that we could see. So as nonchalantly as possible, we walked across the lobby and outside. When we hit the street, Dad started running, repeating over and over, "They're after us! They're after us!"

I tried to hush him up. They would indeed be after us if he kept running and calling out something like that!

A couple of blocks down the street Dad spotted a cop just ahead. "Split!" he called to me. He started one way, and I went the other way.

Sure enough, our running had attracted the attention of that cop, and he started toward us.

At the end of the block, I looked back. The cop had followed Dad. Maybe he thought that Dad was molesting a young girl. Anyway, he wasn't after me.

I ran another block or so and then went into a fast walk, trying not to arouse suspicions. I must have covered ten blocks. When I looked around, I couldn't see the cop, and I didn't see Dad. He had taken off so fast that he didn't tell me where to meet him. So now what? Would he go back to the hotel?

I circled back around, looking for Dad. Block after block, I went looking for him, but I couldn't find him. Had they picked him up?

By this time it was getting dark. Where was I going to stay? I sure wanted to get off the streets. Well, we had already paid for tonight's stay at the hotel. Maybe Dad would meet me back there. But would he be too paranoid to go back? Were the cops really onto us?

Somehow I felt that Dad was being overly suspicious. I couldn't buy his explanation that the maid was really a cop in disguise. So I circled around back to the hotel.

Nobody stopped me when I walked into the lobby. Nobody followed me into the elevator. Nobody tailed me as I walked down the hall to the room we had rented.

I pulled the key out of my pocket. As I opened the door, I called cautiously, "Dad! Dad! Are you here?"

No answer.

I locked the door behind me and waited. In fact, I waited that whole night. I watched TV until about two. Then I fell into an exhausted sleep.

Dad still hadn't shown up by the next morning. Now what was I going to do? It would be useless for me to spend day after day combing the streets for him. But could I feel right about just going off and leaving him without at least trying to find him?

I got a quick breakfast and started my search. But I must have looked suspicious because a police car started following me. Now what?

I made my way into a crowded department store, getting lost among the shoppers. And I was wondering, *Do the police really know about my being here? Is there indeed an all-points bulletin out for my arrest?*

I couldn't take a chance on it. I'd fly back to New York City. At least I knew my way around it a little bit from some of the trips we had made there. And New York City had lots of places to hide if the cops did start closing in on me!

I hailed a taxi and went to the airport. There I got the next flight to New York City, and two hours later I was on a shuttle bus headed toward downtown. I counted my money. I still had two hundred dollars. That would go in a hurry, but at least I wasn't penniless.

I checked into the Holiday Inn on West Fifty-seventh Street. I figured I could last about three days on my money. Then what? I'd have to think about that.

The first day I never left my room. I was hungry, but I was even more scared. When I finally did get nerve enough to go down to the coffee shop, I ate so fast that I got a stomachache.

Then I decided my fear was ridiculous. I had used an alias when flying to New York City. They wouldn't have tailed me here. So I went outside for some fresh air. When I walked by a cop, I figured I'd better test him by staring at him. He simply smiled. He sure didn't suspect anything.

Emboldened by that encounter, I walked to Times Square. A guy came up and asked, "Want some smoke? Coke? Acid?"

I had always avoided drugs; they seemed stupid to me. So I don't really know why I did it, but I said, "Yes, I'll take some pot."

"How many?"

"How much?" I responded.

"A buck a stick."

"Give me three."

I returned to my hotel room with those three sticks, lit up, and got high. It felt like I didn't have a care in the world.

So the next day I walked down to Times Square again—to get some more marijuana. It was no problem finding someone selling it. Pushers were everywhere.

As I headed back to the Holiday Inn, I sensed that someone was following me. I glanced over my shoulder and saw this big guy keeping his distance. I figured he was probably a pimp. They were everywhere, trying to pick up young girls.

I quickened my pace, and so did he. Obviously this

was not my imagination. He *was* following me.

I didn't want to run and arouse some cop's suspicion. After all, not only was I a fugitive, but now I could also be busted for possession.

I quickened my pace again, but he still caught up with me and grabbed my arm.

"Get your filthy hands off me, mister," I yelled, pulling away, "before I call the cops!"

He laughed. "My, aren't you the little tiger!" He said it with all the sarcasm he could muster. "Go ahead and call the cops. They're all friends of mine."

"Are you a detective?" I asked.

He shook his head.

"You think you're somebody big?" I asked.

He laughed again. "Man, I don't think it; I know it! I'm a big man around this town. But what I want to know is what you are doing running away from home."

"What makes you think I'm a runaway?" I snapped. "I live on West Fifty-seventh."

"Sure," he replied. "Could it be you're living at the Holiday Inn—but only until your money runs out?"

How did he know that? Was he really a cop?

"I don't live at the Holiday Inn," I replied. "My mother works there—in the coffee shop."

"And I suppose you live with your mother in room twelve seventeen?"

That was my room number! How in the world did he know that? I looked for a bulge in his upper pocket. That would give him away. If he had a gun there, then I'd know he was a cop. But he looked too slick for a cop. I had to be careful.

I started to walk away from him, but he grabbed my arm again.

"I told you to get your filthy hands off me!" I snapped. "And I mean, now!"

I tried to jerk away again, but this time he was ready

for me. His fingers dug into my arm.

"Listen, baby, nobody talks to me that way and gets by with it," he threatened. "Now I've caught up with you to do you a favor, see? Can you get that through that pretty little thick head of yours?"

I eyed him suspiciously. "And just what kind of a favor do you plan to do for me?"

"I told you, baby, I know all the cops. And I know what they're up to. That means, baby, that I know that they know you're a runaway. In fact, they've got your room staked out. If I were you, I wouldn't go back to the Holiday Inn, room twelve seventeen, or you'll be in big trouble. You'll get picked up and thrown into the slammer. They'll get you for being a runaway; they'll get you for doing drugs. But baby, one way or another, they'll get you. You're in deep trouble!"

What was he getting at? Why would he warn me about the cops? What was in it for him? I'd probably be safer with the cops than I was with him. After all, if the cops were looking for me, it wouldn't be because I was a runaway.

"Get lost!" I told him. "You leave me alone, or I'll fill my mother in on this whole conversation, and she'll go to the authorities!"

I wheeled around and took off toward the hotel. He called after me, "I was only trying to do you a favor, baby. Don't blame me when you get busted!"

At the Holiday Inn I walked cautiously through the lobby. No unusual activity there. I didn't see any police watching my room, either. That guy must have been a pimp trying to scare me into coming with him. He really didn't know anything about me. He suspected I was a runaway. But how did he know my room number? Well, at least I had called his bluff.

I stayed up late watching TV. After all, I didn't have

to get up at the crack of dawn like I did at the training school. And I could choose what I wanted for break-fast—or not eat at all, if that was what I wanted. It sure felt nice being able to make my own decisions.

About midnight my phone rang. I didn't know of a soul who knew I was there.

When I answered, a voice said, "Well, kid, you're still there, huh? Haven't gotten busted yet?"

I recognized his voice and slammed down the re-ceiver.

In minutes the phone rang again. As I answered it, I decided to give him a piece of my mind. But before I could, he shouted, "Listen kid, nobody hangs up on me! Do you understand? Now I know right where you are, so you'd better behave yourself!" His voice sounded so om-inous. I'd better cool it.

"I'm sorry," I said. "It's just that—"

"Save the apologies," he interrupted. "There's no time for that now. All I wanted to do was tell you that the cops are on their way to the Holiday Inn for you. They'll be there within twenty minutes. So baby, grab your stuff and take off while you've got a chance. I'll meet you at the corner of Fifty-sixth and Eighth Avenue. I'm warn-ing you, baby, get out of there while you can. The cops are coming!" Then *click!*

I slowly replaced the receiver. Was that character tell-ing the truth? Or was it another bluff?

I was discovering that it's rough running from the law. You continually wonder if the cops are just outside waiting for you. So I faced the decision again. Where should I go? If the cops came and found me, it would be all over for me—even if they simply thought at this point I was a runaway. It wouldn't take them long to run a record check and realize I was a fugitive.

But maybe that guy was bluffing. He apparently was

bluffing before when he talked to me. If I met him at
Fifty-sixth and Eighth Avenue, then what? Was he a
pimp?

I flopped onto the bed, trying to pull my befuddled
thoughts together. Then I started thinking about prison
and realizing that if they caught me, it would be years
before I got out. I couldn't live through that.

I jumped up and started pacing around the room,
wondering aloud, "What shall I do? What shall I do?" I
walked over to the window and looked down those
twelve floors. Should I open the window and jump?
Maybe then I would find peace. Maybe then nobody
would be hounding me. But then I got to wondering
about what happens when a person dies. Is there such a
place as hell? Would I go there? Was there any truth to
what I had heard Reverend Gossman say at the Community Church the few times I went there? I wondered.

As I stood there in thought, I saw it. A police car
pulled up, and two cops got out! Oh, no! That guy must
have known what he was talking about!

The two cops headed for the lobby. I knew what that
meant. In minutes I'd hear a knock at my door. I had to
get out now—while I could!

I remembered what Dad had said about taking the
fire escape down. No way could I go down on the elevator. I'd run right into the arms of those cops!

Why didn't I check the emergency exits before? I asked
myself as I searched frantically. Then I spotted the sign.
Good thing they required those in public buildings. I
ran to it, pushed open the door, and started down the
stairs. I was glad to be running down, instead of up.
Twelve flights is a long way to go.

Would the emergency stairs enter the lobby? Was
there another way out? Would the cops have the place
surrounded? And if they caught me, would they know
who I really was?

Fortunately I was able to get out into the alley rather than going through the lobby. There were no police guarding the back door. So I took off, running for my life.

I knew of nowhere else to go, so I headed for Fifty-sixth and Eighth. At least I could thank the guy for saving me from the police.

I was almost there when a big arm grabbed me and held me tight. A mugger! I tried to scream, but a big hand slapped over my mouth. Did this mugger plan to rob me? or rape me? or kill me? What a horrible way to die!

When I began to kick and squirm, he said, "Hey, cool it, baby. That's no way to treat a friend. I just saved your life!"

I began to relax as I recognized the voice. At least I wasn't going to be mugged or raped. At least, not now.

He took his hand from my mouth. Completely out of breath, I panted, "Cops almost got me! They were coming to my room!"

He laughed. "See? What did I tell you? If I hadn't called and warned you, those cops would be marching you off in handcuffs right now. You're lucky I called back after you hung up on me. I was so mad about that I almost called the whole thing off. I mean, nobody hangs up on—"

"I said I was sorry," I interrupted. "I mean, a girl can't be too careful, you know."

"That's more like it, baby."

"Okay," I said, "you saved my life. Now what do I owe you?"

He stood there smiling. I knew what was coming next. But he totally disarmed me when he said, "Not a thing, baby; not one thing."

Did he mean it? I was just hoping he wouldn't ask me to do something I'd find totally disgusting. It seemed as though all men had just one thing on their minds.

"You can leave now," he said. "Just walk off. I merely wanted to let you know that any time you need a friend, I'll always be around. But owe me anything? No way, baby. I'm not that kind of a guy."

With that he grabbed my shoulders, spun me around, and faced me away from him, pushing gently on my back. I took a few steps, and he stood there waving at me. "Good-bye, girl. Good-bye," he called.

I moved about ten feet away. Where was I going to go? What was I going to do? Could I go back down to Forty-second Street? Not at this time of night. The people on the streets now were the junkies and the muggers and the pimps. No way would I ever get through that maze alive.

So I turned around, and I said, "Mister, level with me, will you?"

"I did already," he answered. "I'm just a friend who's concerned about a lonely, lost little girl. That's my mission in life. I'm a good guy. Sorry, I forgot to wear my white hat."

I couldn't help but smile at him. He was dressed nicely, rather conservatively, I thought, but nice. And he was certainly a handsome brute. But he just had to be a pimp. I couldn't figure out anything else he would be. And I sure didn't want to get involved with a pimp. No way was I going to go out on the streets and sell my body and let some man live off the earnings!

When I started to walk away again, he called, "Where are you going? Will I see you again?"

"I'm going to Forty-second Street," I announced.

I heard his footsteps running toward me. "For crying out loud!" he shouted. "Don't you have a brain in your head? First I save you from the cops. Now you're heading into something far worse than the cops! Baby, if you go down to Forty-second Street, some pimp is going to grab you so fast it'll make your head spin. There are hundreds of them down there. Any one of them would pounce on you because you would make them millions. Baby, you can't go down to Forty-second Street!"

"Okay, mister, you've got all the answers," I responded. "Where am I going to go?"

12

My question brought a big smile to his handsome face. I knew what was coming.

"Now listen," he started in, "please don't get me wrong. You don't know who I am, and I wouldn't blame you for not trusting me. But I'm going to tell you something. Whether you believe it or not is up to you. But do you know why those cops came to your hotel room?"

Now this was going to be interesting.

"Well, I'll tell you why," he went on when I didn't respond. "For the last few days there's been a pimp tailing you. His name is Boogey Bear."

"Boogey Bear?" I laughed. "That's some name!"

"Well, that is what everybody calls him. His name may be funny, but he is one of the meanest pimps in all of New York City. He's mean, but he's also smart."

"I suppose you're going to tell me that Boogey Bear was coming to get me tonight, but that the cops beat him to the punch. Right?"

"No. Boogey Bear is too smart for that. What he does is tail a runaway until he knows where she's staying. Sometimes he has to bribe a clerk to get her room number. Then he calls the cops and tells them to arrest her, giving them all the details about where she is. The cops will bust her for any number of charges—runaway, vagrancy, drugs, you name it."

"Then good old Boogey Bear comes and bails the poor little girl out of jail. Right?"

"Wrong. He's smart, I told you. What he does is hire a little old lady to go down and make bail. She brings you to Boogey Bear. And you've got to stay with him because if you don't go his way, you go back to jail. And that Boogey Bear is quite a talker. He's got a fancy car, a beautiful apartment, and he gives away gifts like you wouldn't believe. So it isn't long until the girl is going his way, and then he has her out on the streets working for him. He's her pimp."

I couldn't believe what he was telling me. It was bad enough almost getting busted by the cops. But to think it was that dirty pimp who turned me in, trying to turn me into his slave! That was too close for comfort.

"You mean there really is a Boogey Bear?" I asked.

"You'd better believe it. And he's just one of thousands you'll run into around this town—especially if you go down to Forty-second Street."

Why was he telling me all this? What was his game?

"Okay, mister, you've leveled with me so far. But what are you really up to?"

"The name's Lynwood Hart," he said, extending his hand. "I'm just a plain, ordinary citizen in New York City. But I hate pimps. You see, I had a younger sister, Cheryl. She ended up with a pimp. I tried to warn her, but she was so naive. Well, when she finally realized she was his slave, she tried to get away. He killed her."

Lynwood turned away, wiping a tear from his eye.

"At her graveside," he said, facing me again, "I vowed I'd stop every pimp that I could. I've undertaken a personal war against pimps and their unholy business. And it looks like I've just stopped another one."

Once again he brushed a tear from his eye. "She must have been a wonderful sister," I said, as sympathetically as I could. "I'm so sorry it happened to her. But maybe it's lucky for me."

"Yes, I guess you could look at it that way," he agreed. "If I can just stop some of those vicious pimps. . . ." His voice trailed off.

I must be dreaming. How could I be so lucky as to come across the one man in New York City who made it his personal project to stop pimps.

"I have a good job as a stockbroker down on Wall Street," Lynwood went on. "I'm making a lot of money right now. To get the jump on the market, I frequently have to be out at night to check on what's happening overseas. That's what I was doing out tonight."

I didn't hear all he said about his work. I was too busy thinking about the whole situation. I knew New York City was notorious for its pimps. But I had never heard of anyone who made it a project to try to protect innocent girls from those vicious pimps. This sure was some switch!

"Now, I don't want you to think I'm a dirty old man or anything like that," he went on, "but why don't you come to my apartment and stay overnight? I can't let you go down onto Forty-second Street. And you can't go back to the Holiday Inn. Then in the morning we can talk some more and figure out what we're going to do with you. Okay?"

I still didn't know if I could trust him. But taking up his offer seemed a lot better than trying to survive on the street overnight. I knew I'd never live through that.

"It's awfully nice of you to offer me a place to stay," I said. "But let me get something straight. You'd better not try anything!"

He laughed. "Look, you remind me a lot of Cheryl. You can be my little sister. I wouldn't try anything with my sister, would I?"

I told him my first name, and we walked about a
block to where his car was parked. Talk about plush! I'd
never been in such a fantastic car before in all my life. I
guess he was right about making a lot of money.

His apartment was on the Upper West Side, and it
was absolutely divine. When I saw it had two bedrooms,
believe me, I breathed a lot easier.

It was so late that he insisted I go to bed right away.
The bed was so soft and plush; the room so inviting. I
snuggled down under the covers, half-expecting him to
knock on the door at any minute, or to come in unan-
nounced. But he didn't.

When I got up in the morning, he fixed me a big
breakfast. I was beginning to relax a little, and I really
enjoyed it.

As we ate, we talked. He wanted to know about my
family. He seemed so open and helpful that I told him
everything—about my parents, about my record, about
how I had escaped from the state training school, about
Chicago. I knew I really shouldn't have told him all that.
If he were an upright citizen, would he feel it necessary
to call the cops? After all, he could be arrested for har-
boring a fugitive.

Would you believe he just laughed when I told him
about escaping? He thought that stunt my dad pulled
was one of the funniest things he'd ever heard. "I'd sure
like to meet that man," he told me.

I kept waiting for him to excuse himself and go to
work. But he didn't even act as though he were thinking
about leaving. "I'll wash the dishes and clean up the
kitchen," I finally told him. "I know you must have to be
at work by now. And Lynwood, thanks for giving me a
place to stay last night. And thanks for not trying anything. You've been a real friend, and—"

"What do you mean, *been?*" he interrupted. "I'm still
your friend. And I'm not going into the office today. My

job is the kind of thing where I can come and go. In a couple of days I can go down there and get everything caught up. Besides, if I went down there today, you'd be gone before I got back. And that would make me very unhappy."

I blushed a little. Did he really like to be around me? Maybe something would work out. . . .

We goofed off that entire day, talking, laughing, eating. Talk about a contrast to the kind of life I had been living!

That evening he said he had some things to attend to—some business that just couldn't wait. He was kind of vague about it, and I decided it was best for me not to push him. After all, he was doing me a big favor to let me stay there.

I thought maybe he'd be drunk when he came in— like my dad was when he went out at night. But about one when he came back, he was as sober as a judge.

Lynwood told me I could stay as long as I wanted. In fact, he took me out and bought me a whole new wardrobe from some really fine stores. I noticed he paid cash for whatever we bought, and he had a huge wad of bills with him. Whatever he did, he sure made a lot of money at it. Maybe this business of selling stocks was a prosperous business. I needed some kind of a career. I wondered if I were bright enough to get into it.

About a week later Lynwood asked me if I wanted to go for a ride. Of course, I did. We drove down to middle Manhattan—Forty-second and Eighth. He pulled to the curb, and we just sat there for a few minutes. Finally he asked me, "Want to get high?"

"Are you kidding?" I asked.

"No, I get high every once in a while. Not too often, you understand. It's bad for my business. But let me get some stuff, and we'll go back to my apartment and get off. Okay?"

Without waiting for me to answer, he got out, walked up to someone on the street, and made a transaction.

Back at the apartment he told me he'd gotten some cocaine and taught me how to snort it. I got a crazy rush from it. But as I sat there getting high, I noticed Lynwood didn't get off.

I took some cocaine and pushed it toward him. "Come on, man," I said, "snort some. It'll put you beyond the moon!"

He laughed. "No, I'd better not. It's getting too risky for me. I could get my license suspended in the stock market if they caught me taking drugs. But I knew you'd like some. They won't hurt you any."

The following night we went down and bought more drugs—this time heroin. Back at the apartment he prepared it in a hypodermic needle and popped me in the skin.

I really enjoyed that high. And Lynwood seemed to enjoy seeing me that happy. I really forgot all my troubles and problems. So my taking drugs became an every-night affair.

Instead of shooting up one bag, I shot up two bags— every night for about three weeks. I really looked forward to it.

Then one night Lynwood announced, "Sorry, Terri, but no more drugs."

I was disappointed, but I just kind of shrugged. As Lynwood said, they wouldn't hurt anybody. I was a big girl. I could take them or leave them. If he didn't want me to have any more drugs, then I'd quit them. Just like that.

About three hours later, I started getting sick—withdrawal. I had heard other girls talk about it. Now I was experiencing it. And it terrified me.

Lynwood saw what was happening and asked, "Want to get high?"

I jumped up and headed for the door. "Man, do I ever! I'm starting to get sick."

Lynwood pulled me close to him and said, "Baby, I'd really like to get you some drugs, but I'm flat broke. Stocks have really been terrible. I've lost a lot of money, and. . . ."

I began to shudder and shake, getting sicker by the minute. My stomach was rumbling, and I knew that any minute I'd start vomiting. Somehow we had to get some money for those drugs.

"Lynwood," I said, "I am really sorry about your business problems. I wish there were something I could do to make up to you all you've done for me. But right now all I can think about is that I'm going to have to do something to get those drugs. We've got to get some money somewhere."

He pulled me up closer. "Terri, I don't know quite how to say this. No—" He pushed me away.

"What is it? What is it?" I asked eagerly.

Pulling me up next to him again, he said, "I think I know where we can get some quick money. It won't take long."

I didn't ask any questions. All I wanted was to get some money somehow so I could get those drugs.

We drove down to Times Square again and parked. "Stay here," he said. "I'll be right back."

Was he going to get the money and the drugs, too?

In moments he was back—with an older man dressed in a fine suit. He looked like a businessman.

"Terri, this is Mr. Swartz," Lynwood said. "You go with him up to his room and do what he says, and he'll give you a hundred dollars. Okay?"

I stared at Lynwood unbelievingly. He expected me to be a prostitute! No way! I slammed the door.

Then my stomach started churning, and every fiber of my body was aching for those drugs. I just had to have them. I might as well face it. I was hooked. Maybe if I went through with it this time, Lynwood's luck would change and I would never have to do it again.

I opened the door and slid out, mumbling, "Anything you say, Lynwood."

Lynwood smiled. "I know Mr. Swartz will treat you real nice, Terri. He'll be gentle."

I felt like a lamb being led to the slaughter as I walked off with Mr. Swartz toward his hotel room.

"You're a cute little thing," he told me.

I didn't know if he meant it, or if he was just trying to make conversation. Either way, I didn't like the way he said it. The whole thing disgusted me. If it weren't for needing money for drugs, this would be the last thing on earth I would do.

When we got to his room, I was scared to death. I'd heard about sex maniacs and what they did to prostitutes. I had heard about perverts. But most of all, I was hoping this wouldn't take long, because I was getting sicker by the minute.

The man reached into his wallet, pulled out five twenties, and handed them to me. "Your pimp said one hundred dollars, didn't he?" he asked.

I started to explain that Lynwood was no pimp, but I figured it really made no difference. All I was interested in now was in getting this nasty deal over with so I could escape into my drug world. I took the money and tucked it into my bra.

"Okay, let's take care of the business," he said.

I'd never done this before, but I was trapped. I started to vomit, but I swallowed hard. Then I started to unbuttom my blouse.

As I did, he reached into his coat pocket. Oh, no! He was a pervert going for a knife! But he pulled out a wallet, flipped it open, and I stared right at a New York City Police Department badge!

"I'm Detective Farnam, Fifty-fourth Precinct," he said, "and you're under arrest for prostitution."

I edged away, but he grabbed me, spun me around, and had handcuffs on me almost before I knew what was happening.

He read me my rights. Whom would I call? Lynwood? He'd gotten me into this mess. Would he dare come down to bail me out? And why should he?

As we walked down the hall and back to the lobby of the hotel, I kept wondering about whether I should contact Lynwood. I was wondering if he'd be down there waiting for me, and would they pick him up, too? If only there were some way I could warn him. . . .

"We almost got your pimp," Detective Farnam told me as he led me outside. "He's a slippery one, but—"

"Lynwood is no pimp!" I corrected. "He's a nice guy. He wouldn't have done this at all, except that he had run out of money. He knew I had to have money for drugs, and this seemed to him to be the fastest way to get some. He's never done anything like this before, and I've sure never done anything like this before!"

"Maybe you've never done anything like this before," the detective said. "I don't know about that. But I sure know about your pimp. You call him 'Lynwood'? That's not what we know him as."

"You mean his name is not Lynwood Hart?"

"Well," the detective said, "that may be one of his aliases, but we all know him as Boogey Bear. He's one of the most notorious pimps in New York City!"

"Boogey Bear?" I replied. "Oh, no! You've got it all wrong! Lynwood saved me from Boogey Bear!"

"Little girl, you're not very street wise, are you?" the detective said. "I could tell that right away. That Boogey Bear has some of the biggest, fanciest lines you'll ever hear. His latest method is to tail a new girl in town, find out where she's staying, and call the cops to report her as a runaway. Then he calls the girl and tells her to meet him at a certain corner because the cops are closing in on her. She literally runs into his clutches! One of these days we're going to nail that guy and nail him good!"

I couldn't believe it. For more than three weeks now I had been living with Boogey Bear! I should have remembered what Dad had always told me: There's no such thing as a free lunch!

Detective Farnam took me to the police station, where I was booked, fingerprinted, and had a mug shot taken. They stuck me in a cell and told me that tomorrow I would be taken down and arraigned on the prostitution charge.

That wasn't what was worrying me most. When they started comparing fingerprints, they'd find out who I really was!

I was too sick to sleep that night. The bunk was a hard board with no blanket. The only furnishing in the cell was a roll of toilet tissue.

I sat there on that bunk, miserable, hating myself and the life I had lived. My whole world caved in, and I started to weep. Didn't anyone care about me? If there were a God, why did He let all these things happen to me?

The following morning I saw two couples and an officer coming down the hallway. I overheard the man say, "This is where we shot *Teenage Runaway.*"

They left, and I wondered about what they had said. I guessed they were talking about making a movie. I felt reasonably certain that no one would shoot a teenage runaway, not even at the state training school! But I wondered why would anybody shoot a movie in a place like this.

When the officer walked by again a few minutes later, I said, "Excuse me, sir. Who were those people?"

"Oh, that was Reverend Benton and his wife, Elsie. The other couple was the Metzgers. Reverend Benton wanted them to see what our jail looked like. They shot part of a movie here."

"Oh?" I asked. "Are ministers making movies these days?"

"Well, Reverend and Mrs. Benton have a home for delinquent girls upstate at Garrison. They care for girls who are addicts, alcoholics, prostitutes—any girls in trouble. They've been able to help a great many girls. They make these films as a way of helping other girls. The Bentons are really wonderful people."

"Wonderful people?" I said in scorn. "I don't think there are any wonderful people in this world."

The officer grunted and turned away. I went back and sat down. What wonderful people had I ever known? The closest was Lynwood—and he turned out to be Boogey Bear. All along that pimp was working around to putting me out on the streets! He hooked me on drugs so I'd do whatever he suggested. That dirty so-and-so, if I ever got out of here, I was going to look him up and. . . .

Get out of here? Why was I kidding myself? They'd probably already found out who I really was. I'd be headed to prison for a long, long time. I couldn't take that!

I looked around that cell for something I could use to hang myself. There was no hope for me now.

My search was interrupted by the sound of footsteps approaching. It was a woman—one of the women who had been there earlier with the group. She walked up to my cell and said, "When I was by here a few minutes ago, I noticed you. I felt so burdened and concerned for you that I spoke with Lieutenant Collins and got permission to come back and talk with you. Do you need help?"

Who was this woman? And why did she want to help me?

"Who are you?" I asked suspiciously. At the moment I wasn't very big on trusting anybody.

She smiled—such a big, beautiful smile. "They call me Mom B," she said. "My husband, John Benton, and I are directors of the Walter Hoving Home in Garrison. It's a home for girls like you."

"Like me?" I asked. "But I'm a drug addict, and I just got busted for prostitution, and—"

She extended her hand through the bars and tried to pull me toward her. "Honey," she said, " I know all that. And I just wish these bars didn't separate us. I think you need a big hug right about now—someone to love and understand you. More than that, you need Jesus to heal your hurts and make you a different person."

She tried to push her face through the bars. "This is not going to work," she finally said. "Just a minute; I'll be right back."

I wasn't going anywhere.

I eagerly awaited her return. There was something different about this woman. Somehow I sensed she had something I needed.

In minutes she returned with a matron who unlocked my cell, and Mom B got in with me. It didn't seem to bother her that she was locked in there with me. In fact, without saying anything, she just grabbed me and hugged me close. "I could tell you needed a big hug," she said, patting me. I found myself buried in her arms, and it felt so good.

It's hard to describe what happened next. Inside it felt like a dam broke, and I began to weep uncontrollably. I looked up at her through my tears, and saw she was crying, too.

As she gently wiped the tears from my eyes, she said, "I hope you don't think I'm too forward. But when I meet a girl like you, I just have to hug her and tell her about Jesus and how He loves her. After all the terrible disappointments you've had in life, Jesus wants to give you a real turnaround, a real reason for living."

Then she asked my name. "Terri," she said, "why don't we sit down over there? I want to share something with you. It's so powerful and exciting that it can change your whole life!"

We sat down together, and she pulled a little black book out of her purse. "This is called the New Testament," she said. "It has the answers to life's problems."

As I looked at it, memories of Sunday school came back. I recognized it; it was part of the Bible.

Mom B opened her Bible and explained something I shall never forget as long as I live. She showed me from the Bible that I was a sinner. The things I had done wrong in my life were the result of sin. She gently told me that if I would confess my sins to Jesus and ask Him for forgiveness, my whole life would be changed. She made it so convincing, so logical, so simple. And I believed.

She invited me to follow her in what she called the sinner's prayer. In that prayer, very simply I asked Jesus to forgive all my sins. As I confessed them to Him, I really did believe that He forgave them all, just like the Bible said. Then Mom B asked me to accept Jesus into my heart by faith. So again very simply I said, "Jesus, please come into my heart."

After we got through that prayer, Mom B asked me, "Now, Terri, where is Jesus?"

First, I wondered what she meant. Then I thought about what we had just prayed. "Well, according to what I just prayed," I said, "He's in my heart."

She slapped me joyfully on one shoulder and declared, "That's right, Terri! That's where He is! And He'll always be there as long as you let Him stay!"

I was so excited I threw my arms around her and hugged her.

"Terri," she told me, "the reason I can love you and you can love me, even though we are practically strangers to each other, is because of the love of Jesus. His love makes us love one another."

I could believe it. I'd never felt like this before!

She stood up and called the matron. But as she left, she said, "I'll be back."

As I saw her disappear down the hall, I wondered if she would ever come back. Was I dreaming? If I were, it sure felt good! I felt like a completely new person!

In a few minutes Mom B did come back, this time with an officer. She was almost bubbling over as she told me, "Good news, Terri! God has performed another miracle. My husband and I just spoke with the authorities here, and they have agreed to drop the charges against you if you would come up to Garrison with us."

"What?" I asked in shock. "You did what?"

"I didn't do anything," she said, giving me that big smile. "The Lord did it. They'll drop the charges against you if you come with us."

I took a big leap and threw myself into Mom B's arms. "Tell me I'm not dreaming!" I said. "I'll go! I'll go!"

"Young lady, you are very fortunate," the officer said. "God must be on your side. This is not at all our normal procedure. But because the Bentons are such good friends of this precinct and because we know they are able to help girls like you, we decided we would try this approach. You're really lucky."

Before I realized what I was doing, I had squeezed that cop. Can you imagine a cop hater like me hugging one?

Mom B put her arm around me and led me down the hallway. I had to sign some papers, and then once again

I was out on the street. There she introduced me to her husband and to the Metzgers. Then we got into their car.

When we pulled into the grounds of the Walter Hoving Home, I knew for sure I must have died and gone to heaven. It was such a beautiful estate that had been made into a haven for girls like me. Reverend Benton—the girls call him Brother B—shared with me how the Lord had miraculously given them this home and how Christians all across the country helped support its ministry. "This is a place of miracles," he told me. And now I was entering this miracle, too!

I learned their program was for a year. We spent a lot of time studying the Bible and learning how to live. It was exciting.

I was encouraged to contact my parents. When I called Mom and told her where I was and what had happened to me, she was almost beside herself. "Praise the Lord! Praise the Lord!" she kept saying over and over. Then I remembered that Dad had once said Mom had gotten religion. Well, she didn't just get religion. She got Jesus!

I learned from her that Dad had made it home from Chicago. Apparently the authorities hadn't suspected his part in the escape and hadn't really bothered him.

Mom and Dad even drove up to visit me. As soon as I grabbed Mom, I knew things were different. She was my real mother now, and I was her real daughter. Jesus made the difference.

Mom and Dad stayed at Garrison overnight. That evening Mom B took them to the basement prayer room. When they came upstairs again, I knew something had happened. Dad had been crying.

"Terri, your father has something to tell you," Mom B said.

Dad looked at me and started to cry again. Then he blurted it out: "Terri, I have just given my life to Jesus. I

did it once before when I was younger. Now I'm really
going to stay with it!"

I threw my arms around him, and Mom threw her
arms around both of us. Then Mom B got into the act as
all of us began to weep—only these were tears of joy.
We were a Christian family!

While I was at the Home, I told Brother B about my
escape from the state training school. He didn't tell me I
had to go to the authorities; but I knew I would never
have complete freedom until I did. I prayed a lot about
it, realizing that I might have to go back to prison. But I
knew that I could face it now; I could take Jesus with
me. And He made all the difference!

Would you believe that the court let me go free? The
authorities looked carefully at my record at the Walter
Hoving Home and said I had made such fantastic
progress, they could see no purpose being served in
making me go back to jail.

Dad also confessed his part in the escape plot. The authorities didn't seem too surprised. They had found his
car stuck in the mud near the railroad tracks and had
traced its registration to him. I got the distinct im-
pression that not all the authorities were happy with the
personnel or the methods of that institution but were
powerless to do much about it. Apparently it had become known that the pattern at the training school was
to provoke girls into doing things that necessitated
longer sentences.

Anyway, their attitude contributed to another miracle
for Dad and me. No longer did we have to live under a
shadow.

Not only was I given spiritual training at the Walter
Hoving Home, I was also able to finish my high-school
studies. The Home has a school that is recognized by the
New York State Department of Education.

I discovered that when I found Jesus, I also found a

greater zest for living, a purpose in it all. I decided that whatever I did, I would try to do my best, for the glory and honor of God. Now that I had a reason for living, I made excellent grades.

I felt so gratified at the end of that year as I graduated from the program at the Walter Hoving Home. Mom and Dad were there, beaming with pride. My, God had certainly been merciful to us!

Now I am in Evangel College in Springfield, Missouri, studying to become a chaplain. When I graduate from college, I intend to go to seminary. Then I'll move back to New York City where I will be working with the Walter Hoving Home. They have a crisis center in New York City. I want to become an official chaplain, ministering to those in jails and visiting the emergency rooms of the hospitals—that's where a lot of junkies go when they overdose. I want to be there to reach them with the love of Christ—just like Mom B was there to reach me.

I have another secret ambition. I'll be looking for Lynwood—or Boogey Bear. This time I've got something for him—something more powerful than anything he's ever come up against before. I want to tell him about the love of Christ! That pimp really needs to know Jesus.

But what about you? Are you looking for happiness but can't seem to find it? Has life dealt you a dirty trick? Has it been totally unfair?

That's the way I viewed it. But I found out differently. I found out that without the Lord, life is always difficult. And only with Him does it make sense.

Do you want to find joy and peace like I did? All you have to do is ask Jesus to forgive you of your sins. He will. Then by faith receive Him into your heart. Now don't worry about how you feel. Sometimes feelings will happen; sometimes they won't. I had tremendous feelings of joy and relief. But I've talked to others who said

they really didn't feel anything at first. That's why I say
it doesn't happen because of how you feel; it happens
because you have faith in Jesus and in His Word, the
Bible.

In the Bible Jesus said that He stands at the door of
your heart and knocks. If you open the door, He will
come in. Won't you do it now? Invite Him in by faith.
He will come in, and from that point on He will be your
Saviour and Lord of your life.

I do hope you will make that decision right now.
You'll never be sorry.

I'm praying you will do it. That decision will be the
beginning of a life of miracles for you. I know. Look
what happened to me!

The Walter Hoving Home.

Some good things are happening at The Walter Hoving Home.

Dramatic and beautiful changes have been taking place in the lives of many girls since the Home began in 1967. Ninety-four percent of the graduates who have come with problems such as narcotic addiction, alcoholism and delinquency have found release and happiness in a new way of living—with Christ. The continued success of this work is made possible through contributions from individuals who are concerned about helping a girl gain freedom from enslaving habits. Will you join with us in this work by sending a check?